MW01274573

The Master's Calling

By

Amber Schamel

©2015 by Amber Schamel
http://www.AmberSchamel.com
Published by Vision Writer Publications
200 S. Wilcox St. #328
Castle Rock, CO 80104

Paperback edition created 2015

All rights reserved. No part of this publication may be
reproduced, stored in a retrieval system, or transmitted in any
form, or by any means –for example, electronic, photocopying,
recording—without the prior written consent of the publisher.
The only exception is brief quotations in printed reviews. This
eBook is licensed for your personal enjoyment only. This eBook
may not be sold or given away to other people. If you would like
to share this book with another person, please purchase an
additional copy for each recipient. If you're reading this book
and did not purchase it, or it was not purchased for your use
only, please return to Amazon and purchase your own copy.
Thank you for respecting the hard work of this author.

This book is a work of fiction. The names, characters, places,
and incidents are products of the writer's imagination or have
been used fictitiously and are not to be construed as real. Any
resemblance to persons, living or dead, actual events, locales or
organizations is entirely coincidental.

All Scriptures quotations are taken from the King James
Version (Public Domain).

Cover Design by Cynthia Hickey.

Photos from Adobe Stock Photos and Schamel's Legacy
Photography.

Acknowledgements

First of all, I would like to thank my Lord and Savior, Jesus Christ. He is the real Author, I am merely a vessel. I have seen His hand at work every step of the way, guiding me through Malon's journey and dropping hints when I get stuck. In truth, the only thing that's good in me is Jesus.

I would also like to thank my family. My dad, my mom, my 11 siblings, and all of my family who have been so supportive and understanding through this process. My parents have provided mentorship and guidance through this process which has been priceless. My mom is my Brainstorming Buddy and helps me hash out my stories before they go on the page. She is a big part of the story formation. Dad, thank you for your thoughts and encouragement. Your input makes the story so much more powerful!

My critique partners, Joy Avery Melville, Susan Karsten, my editor Deidre Lockhart and so many others have helped make this story into what it is. I am so thankful for each of these individuals! The wonderful ladies at Seekerville, and the members of ACFW have taught me so much! I cannot thank them enough for the investment that they've made into my life and writing.

But most of all, a HUGE THANK YOU to all of my friends and readers! This project would be impossible without your support! Thank you for caring, reading, sharing, and your encouraging words. The fact that you would take time out of your day to read my work or send me a comment is such an honor for me. By sharing these stories with your friends, you have given me the greatest compliment possible.

THANK YOU!

Author's Note

I am so excited for you to join me in Malon's adventure! This is a work of Biblical fiction. Though many of the events and characters are fictitious, I have taken pains to stay as close as possible to the Biblical and historical accounts of events, and stay true to the characters portrayed in the Scriptures. If you would like to read the actual accounts of events woven through this book, you can read them in the Gospel of John and the Acts of the Apostles.

I have included a Glossary & Pronunciation Guide at the back of this book. This glossary contains Hebrew words and names along with a definition and pronunciation for your reading pleasure. If at any time you run across a word you do not understand, a character you do not recognize, or a name you can't pronounce, just flip to the glossary to find out.

Again, thank you so much for joining me in this adventure! My prayer is that it will be a great blessing to you, and bring the Bible to life in a way you've never experienced before.

If you don't already know me, I would love to meet you! You can find me on the Stitches Thru Time blog, on my website, and on all of the main social media sites.

Blessings,

Amber Schamel

Bringing HIStory to Life

http://amberschamel.com/

Blogs: http://www.stitchesthrutime.blogspot.com

http://www.hhhistory.com

Facebook -

https://www.facebook.com/AuthorAmberSchamel

Twitter: @AmberSchamel

Pintrest - http://pinterest.com/AmberDSchamel/

Goodreads -

https://www.goodreads.com/author/show/7073165.Amber
_Schamel

Chapter One

Circa 33 A.D.

Malon's heart stopped as an agonized scream pierced the Galilean sky.

Imah.

The goods he'd been carrying clattered to the cobblestone street. Panic seized him while he raced toward the villa. His father's footsteps echoed in the courtyard behind him.

"Imah, where are you?"

Clay shattered in the kitchen. A groan followed. His mother crumpled on the floor, clutching her swollen belly. Malon skidded to a stop, and his father ran into him, nearly sprawling him on top of her.

"Aaliyah." Abba knelt and cradled her head in his lap.

"It...came on...so fast." She gasped.

"Malon, go for Savta and the midwife. As fast as you can run!" Scooping Imah into his arms, Abba hastened to the bedchamber.

Malon bolted through the courtyard and out into the street. Abba would have to deliver the babe unless Malon fetched the midwife in time. He flew down the main street, tripping over children and leaving disgruntled street peddlers in his wake. Turning a corner, he rammed into something big and hard. Dazed, he stumbled backward and glared at the offending object.

A tall Roman centurion glowered back at him, his plumed helmet cockeyed, and the bag he'd been carrying strewn at his feet. He righted his helmet. "What do you think you're doing, boy?"

Malon drew himself to his full height. He was more than sixteen now, a man by Jewish terms. "I beg your pardon, Centurion. Please excuse me. I have no time to argue."

He winced the moment those words left his mouth.

The centurion's eyes narrowed even further, and his big hand reached out and grasped Malon's tunic. "You dare address a centurion this way? Somebody needs to teach you a lesson."

"Please, my mother is in labor. If I don't bring the

midwife quickly, she'll deliver without her."

The centurion sneered. "Well now, what are you going to do when your mother has another babe to suckle?"

Oh, if Israel were not under Roman rule. Malon gritted his teeth. Hard. Pain shot up his jaw and into his temples.

"Very well then, if you will pay the proper respect to a centurion of the Imperial Army, I will let you go." The centurion jerked on Malon's tunic, and his knees met the street with bruising force. "There. That's where you Jews belong."

Malon inhaled against the pain and anger uniting inside him. "Please let me go. My mother—"

"The day is hot, and I need to travel to Tiberius. I'm compelling you to carry my belongings for the first mile."

Of all the times for a Roman to compel him for a mile. Of all the lads in this city. Why did it have to be him…now? Had it not been for his mother writhing in pain, her every hope pinned on him, he would have obliged the soldier. After all, a citizen of Judea had no choice.

He'd have to find a way out. "I'm sorry, Centurion, I am unable to help you at this time. If you would like to wait—"

"Wait? You're obligated by Roman law to carry this pack for me." He shoved the heavy bag into Malon's chest.

"You will do it."

One more cause to hate Romans. There was no reason to them, only selfish pride. Malon grasped the bag and feigned his best look of submission. Maybe he'd pass the midwife's house along the way. "Very well, Centurion."

With a smirk, the soldier grabbed his arm and pulled him along — in the opposite direction of the midwife's house. "Wise of you. Come on, lad."

Malon matched pace with the centurion. After a moment, the soldier released his arm, and Malon fell into step behind him. This was the opportunity he'd hoped for. No telling what the Roman would do to him afterward, but if he could outrun the soldier in all his array, he could summon the midwife before getting caught. Dropping the centurion's bag, Malon bolted toward the midwife's hut. The pumping of his heart echoed his footsteps.

"Get back here, boy! I'll have you flogged!"

He raced on. The breath tore through his lungs, and dust prickled his shins as he ran faster than he ever had before. Running from a Roman centurion infused a new strength into his limbs. If it cost him his life, he'd succeed for his imah. His nostrils burned, and hair tickled his ears. He reached the midwife's dwelling and threw himself at the latch. The door gave way, and he fell inside, announced by a startled shriek.

Spitting the dust out of his mouth, he spotted the old woman crouching behind a stool. "Shiphrah!"

"Malon? Is it you?"

"My imah is in travail. You must come quick. It came on fast."

The midwife jumped from her hiding place and scurried around the room, gathering objects into a scarf. "Is your imah alone?"

Malon pushed himself into a sitting position and gasped to catch his breath. "No, Abba is with her."

A few wrinkles smoothed from the woman's forehead, but she still worked in haste. "I'm ready. Let us go."

He nodded. Though his lungs ached for air, he forced himself up and followed her out of the door. As soon as he stepped into the street, a hand grabbed his shoulder.

"You." The centurion panted, blowing puffs of foul breath into his face. "You…will pay…for this."

"Malon?" The midwife's brow puckered, and she stepped toward him.

"No, Shiphrah. Go to my mother. I will be fine as long as I know Imah and the babe are looked after." He forced a smile to convince her.

With a frown and nod, she scuttled away.

Tightening the grip on Malon's shoulder, the centurion turned. "Soldier!" Two patrolmen snapped to attention. "Take this boy to the post. I compelled him to bear my burden, and he refused. Ten lashes should make him more willing and teach him a little respect."

The soldiers stationed themselves on either side of Malon and grasped his arms, only then did the centurion release the talon grip on his shoulder. "Let's go, boy."

Malon went without resistance. Sometimes, a price must be paid, and today, it was worth it. By the time he got home, he'd have a little brother or sister and overjoyed parents. HaShem was good. Someday, HaShem would free them from this miserable oppression. Someday soon. The Messiah was walking among them, waiting for the right time.

East of the town, the Roman garrison's black towers came into view. It rose like the residence of evil itself with its basalt walls, sharp points, and soldiers swarming it like ants. The garrison cast a dark shadow over a courtyard with the whipping post often used to punish minor crimes. Many times Malon had passed by whilst they administered lashes. He'd shuddered at the cries of men unfortunate enough to be caught.

The soldiers yanked him toward the post, and it grew into a giant as they drew near. His eyes traveled up the post until it stabbed the blue sky. One of the guards shoved his shoulder, ramming him into the post, and raised his arms above his head. They fastened his wrists inside metal clasps attached to the post, then stepped away.

The centurion stared at him for long moments, breathing in heavy puffs, before he snatched up the whip and strode toward him. He unraveled the long leather cord and gave it a jerk. A thunderous crack ricocheted off the black walls.

Malon leaned his forehead against the pole. The centurion said ten lashes. Was that the protocol? Or would the centurion beat him until he decided to stop?

Sweat trickled down his chest. Why did nervous sweat smell so bad? If his hands were free, he would've covered his ears. Though it wouldn't have helped. The cries he heard were in his memory and could not be silenced. He wouldn't be like the guilty thieves and scoundrels who usually stood at this post. He'd take the lashes like a man. Balling his fists, he waited.

The centurion's footsteps circled him, with an occasional pop of the lash. Tyrannical…insane…he couldn't think of a word strong enough to describe the snake. Romans feasted on intimidation, and this centurion was ten times worse than the typical.

"Shouldn't you be in a hurry, Centurion? You have yet to travel to Tiberius."

A low sound rumbled behind him, either a chuckle or a growl. "If you knew what was coming to you, boy, you wouldn't be so anxious."

The lash tore through Malon's tunic and into his flesh. Air escaped his lungs in a high-pitched groan.

The centurion laughed. "The little suckling won't even get to run home to his mother when we're through. You're still going to carry my pack, boy."

The insult intensified Malon's determination and dulled the pain. He could endure ten lashes.

One.

Another crack, but this time, he clenched his teeth to keep from making a sound.

Two.

He tightened his fists and set his jaw. He'd show these pathetic Romans what a real man looked like. He'd endure their cruelty and carry the pack, all without a word of complaint.

Three.

Pain slashed across his back, and a slight breeze sieved through the shreds of his tunic.

Four.

He spread his legs and braced against the pole.

Five. Halfway done.

The courtyard had fallen silent. Were other soldiers

watching, or was he alone with only the outraged centurion?

Six, seven, eight.

The next three lashes came in a quick burst. Then it stopped.

Malon let out the breath he'd been holding and closed his eyes.

The centurion's footsteps paused next to him. "It seems our whip isn't good enough for a prideful boy." Putrid breath accompanied the words. He pivoted on his heel and stalked out of sight. Chains rattled against the wooden table...metal glided...and something whistled through the air. The centurion grunted, as if he'd found something else suitable. Whatever he tried next, Malon would take in silence.

Only two more lashes. Would the centurion really stop at ten? If they were alone in the courtyard, who would prevent him? The centurion may beat him until he begged for mercy, and he'd die first. Malon licked blood off his lip. He'd done nothing wrong.

Something whistled through the air, caught the base of Malon's head, and lacerated his entire back. Agony reverberated through his whole body.

"How does that feel, you sniveling Jew?" This time, spittle accompanied the centurion's bad breath.

Adonai, give me the strength to endure this, and cause Your Messiah to rise soon.

"One more…Centurion. Then let's be on…our way." Malon grimaced from the labored sound in his voice.

The centurion delivered one last blow with the…whatever it was. And Malon started breathing again. He peered behind him as the centurion raised a spiked rod for another blow.

"Gallus, if you wish the boy to carry your pack, you best leave him in the condition to do so. You've carried out his sentence. Now let him go." The deep voice stilled the centurion's hand.

Gallus, so that was the wicked man's name.

With a scowl, Gallus threw down the rod and waved toward Malon. "Loose him."

When his wrists were free, Malon shifted to see who came to his aide. Another centurion leaned against the stone wall, his helmet under his arm. He looked familiar, but with blood and sweat blurring his vision, Malon couldn't tell.

"Your favoritism of the Jews will be your demise, Vitalis." Gallus addressed the other centurion.

Malon knew that name. He'd remember the name of Centurion Dexius Vitalis forever. Twice now, the man had saved him—first from the outlaw Barabbas and now from

Gallus.

"The Jews are our subjects, not our enemies. There is a difference. You would do well to remember." How Vitalis could speak so calmly to such vermin, Malon didn't know.

Shaking his head, Gallus strode over and gripped Malon's arm. "Are you ready to bear my burden now, boy?"

Gallus had little right to call him a boy, but Malon swallowed his irritation. "You need not force me."

Gallus laughed. Heartily. All the way to the city gate, this time walking behind Malon. As soon as they passed through the gates, Malon began counting. He was obligated to serve this monster of a man one thousand steps. Then he could go home. Had the midwife arrived in time? Was Imah well? Was the child a boy or a girl? Whatever the answers, he had one thousand steps before he could find out.

Soon his arms muscles began to burn. Usually, he'd carry such a burden on his back. Not now. At five hundred steps, he almost lost count from trying to shift the weight in his arms. He stumbled, and Gallus' giant hand delivered a blow to his tattered back.

"No foolishness, boy. You're only halfway."

Each step became more and more painful. The jostling movement stretched and tore the scabs on his back and sides, irritating the wounds. The last hundred steps were sheer torture. The sun beamed down on him, scorching his skin and leaching any remaining moisture from his body. Parched and gasping for breath, he reached the count.

"One thousand." He slammed the pack onto the ground and spit the dirt out of his mouth.

"Well done, boy. I'll be sure to find you next time I'm traveling."

He could have slapped the smirk from Gallus' face. Words rose up from deep within and flowed out of his mouth before he could stop them. "One day, Roman, you will be powerless. One day you will not be able to compel me any longer. A deliverer is coming, and then you will have no command over me."

Good thing Gallus didn't have a whip, or he may have finished what he intended to do earlier. Not waiting for his anger to unleash, Malon spun and sprinted home as quickly as his ragged body permitted. He had not just a father waiting for him, but his mother, and now, a newborn brother or sister.

Chapter Two

"Malon, you're safe." The midwife threw open the courtyard gate and enveloped him in a suffocating embrace. "Adonai be praised. I was so worried when that ugly centurion dragged you away."

He bit his lip against the pain of her touch and choked words past the stifled cry in his throat. "Is Imah well?"

"Very well, thanks to you. I got here just in time. The babe came minutes after I arrived. Your poor abba was so relieved." The woman gave a hearty laugh. "Well, what are you waiting for? Go in and meet your baby sister."

"Sister?"

"Why, yes. It is a girl."

His expression must have been humorous, because Shiphrah laughed again. Why did it seem everyone was laughing at him today? When he took a step forward, her smile vanished. She rested a nurturing hand on his. "Are you hurt?"

"I'll be fine." He tried to move past her. Foolish move.

She let out a gasp and clutched his tattered tunic. "What did that monster do to you? Oh, you poor boy."

"I am not a boy." He jerked from her grasp and limped toward his parent's chamber. He'd been called a boy far too many times today, but instant remorse slapped him over treating the elderly woman that way. He attempted a smile over his shoulder. "I'll be fine. I wish to see my sister."

As he approached his parent's bedchamber, the wooden door swung open. "Malon? Praise be to HaShem. The midwife came, but you were not with her. She said you'd been taken by a centurion. I wanted to come after you, but I couldn't leave your mother. I'm so glad you're safe."

Abba tugged him close, and for a moment, Malon thought he wouldn't let go. Pain scattered across his back at Abba's touch, and he couldn't contain the sharp intake of breath.

Abba pulled back, a frown contorting his beard. "You're hurt."

"I'll be all right."

Abba placed his hands on Malon's shoulders and

turned him around. A long moment of silence ensued. "The Romans did this to you?"

"In my haste to fetch the midwife, I plowed into a centurion. He decided he wanted to compel me to carry his pack. I told him he'd have to wait or find someone else, and that angered him. I outran him and got to the midwife in time, so it was worth it."

Abba gritted his teeth. "Romans have no compassion or sense. They're a bloody people, and soon all the blood they have spilt will be returned upon their own heads, tenfold."

"Yes, Abba. Jesus will rise against them soon. I know he will." Malon's spirits lifted at the thought, and his chin followed.

"We need to get these wounds treated."

He twisted to see past Abba into the room. "I wish to meet my sister."

A tender smile softened his father's face. "Of course. Come in."

Stepping inside the dim chamber, Malon grinned at his mother. She sat propped up on the bed, her hair cascading like an embrace from behind. Her skin glistened with perspiration, and her movements were slow and weary. But even fatigue couldn't disguise the joy overflowing from her eyes. Her face beamed as she held out her hand. "Come, my son. Meet your baby sister."

He glanced at Abba, who gave him an approving nod, then walked to her side.

Her fingers felt cold as she squeezed his hands. "See the gift Adonai has given to me? He restored my health, my husband, and my son. Then He went beyond all hopes and gave me more than I had dared to ask for."

She lifted her elbow that he might see the babe's face. It was so small, so round. Fat little lips puckered at the movement. Dark lashes lined closed eyelids, and a dusting of dark hair covered her head. As gently as he could, he traced her cheek, feather soft beneath his touch. She smiled when his finger rounded her chin.

Imah laughed softly. "It seems she's ticklish."

Abba perched on the edge of the bed and, with misty eyes, peered at the newborn. For several moments, no one said anything. Too awestruck to form words.

When at last Malon loosed his tongue, he asked the question that had been begging for an answer since he entered. "How do you call her?"

Imah looked at Abba, and her eyes searched his. "Her name is Topaz."

*****

"Malon, where is the last bottle of ink? It was on this shelf yesterday, and I cannot find it now."

"I sold it last night, Abba, before I locked up."

Abba gave a sarcastic sigh. "You sell too much, my boy. How is an old man to keep up with you?"

"You're not an old man yet." Malon quirked his brow. "You have a newborn babe. You're practically a newlywed again."

His father's laughter followed him outside the shop. Malon folded the display blankets and packed them away in the crate. When he'd dismantled the outdoor displays, he grabbed an empty crate and headed back inside. Kish was recounting the money and checking the logs, while Abba called out the remaining inventory from the shelves.

Malon dropped the crate, and a swirl of dust ascended. He stretched his arms above his head, moving slowly and wincing as the movement tugged at his healing stripes. "Abba, what else do we require for the feast tomorrow?"

"Three more clay jars, six more candles, and see if you can find the bowl that came in from Ostia."

"We need more oil for the lamps as well, do we not?"

"No. We will get that on the way home."

"On the way home?" Malon frowned. "Where do you intend to get it?"

"From your Uncle Noah."

"Uncle Noah? Abba, you haven't spoken to him since Imah fell ill."

"I know, and now it is time to right the wrongs. Noah was right about your mother, and I treated him cruelly. It is time for me to swallow my pride and say what he has needed to hear these many years." Abba swallowed hard. "Did you log the supplies we are taking, Kish?"

"Yes, sir, but I have a few more entries to check. You and Malon can go ahead. I'll finish here."

Abba patted Kish's shoulder. He'd been an apprentice for many years, but now was working hard to earn a share of the company. Having Kish there to help Abba and take over the trade pleased Malon. While he liked the business, when the time came for Jesus to make his stand as Messiah, Malon intended to join him.

Shouldering the crate of goods Abba had dictated, Malon ignored his aching back and followed his father across the empty market toward Uncle Noah's oil press. The sinking sun's red glow added to the foreboding growl of his stomach. He still recalled the night Abba and Uncle Noah quarreled all those years ago. Noah was actually Imah's uncle, but that didn't keep him from being a favorite of Malon's. The jolly man always had a treat for him as a boy, but he had ceased to be a part of their lives after he stormed out of their house, leaving embarrassment where there had been a joyous feast. It must have been something about Imah, because the incident happened not long after she became ill and had to leave. Abba refused to speak of it, so Malon never knew for certain.

The olive press was no longer running, and the donkey had been unhitched and nibbled at the straw on the ground. The scent of olives permeated the air, and the crushing stone still glistened from the day's press.

Abba approached the small shop and tapped on the wooden door. "Noah, are you still here?"

Footsteps clomped inside. Then the door jerked open. Uncle Noah's blue eyes widened, deepening the wrinkles on his forehead. His white beard parted as his mouth dropped open, and then settled into a frown. What made him look so different from how Malon remembered him? "What do you want, Ben-Adamiel? We're closed."

"My business is twofold. I am in need of some oil, but I also hoped you would spare a moment to speak with me."

"You've done enough talking to last a lifetime. We're closed."

Noah started to slam the door, but Abba's hand prevented him. "Please, Noah. I must apologize."

"Apologize?" The door swung open, and Uncle Noah

crossed his arms over his plump middle. "Very well, apologize."

Abba took a deep breath, and the lump in his throat bobbed — swallowing his pride? Malon smirked.

"I was wrong about Aaliyah, and I mistreated her. I also wronged you. I should never have said what I did, and I am asking you to forgive me. Please know I was acting on the facts I had at the time and in my family's best interest."

"It was in Aaliyah's best interest for you to throw her into the street? To spread rumors about her character?"

"She had severe leprosy. What else was I to do? She could not stay. The law requires her to separate."

"You didn't have to call her an adulteress."

Abba held up his hands. "The priests believed the disease was to judge her for her sin."

"You could have at least visited her at the colony." Noah sniffed as he lifted his chin.

"How many times did you visit her, Noah?"

"Well...I...At least I sent food for her."

"I am admitting my actions were wrong. Terribly wrong. Now I am asking your forgiveness."

What a shock to see how much the old man had changed. Malon remembered Uncle Noah as a jovial man, full of life, with his thick white beard. Now all light had seeped from his eyes above his scraggly beard.

"I also wanted to invite you to the feast we are holding tomorrow to celebrate the birth of our daughter."

"Y-your...your daughter? Aaliyah had another child?"

"Yes. Her days of purification have passed, and now we wish to celebrate with our friends and family. As I recall, you are both."

A corner of Noah's mouth lifted. "It would be so good to see Aaliyah well and with a baby. What of you, my boy?" The old man extended a hand to Malon. "My, you have grown."

"Yes, sir." Malon smiled. At least some of the old happiness had returned to his uncle's manner. "So you will come? I'd like it very much, and I know Imah would too."

"Very well. I will come, and I will send a vat of oil to your home first thing in the morning."

A thrill danced through Malon's chest, but Abba's face tightened. "Wonderful. Our family will be expecting you."

*****

Excitement buzzed through the Ben-Adamiel household as guests began to arrive for the dedicational feast. Fishermen in plain clothing, merchants in lush robes, even priests with their tassels and headdresses, crowded the courtyard of their villa. The music of harps and flutes echoed off the stone walls. The guests laughed, talked, and partook of the scrumptious treats the servants had prepared. Malon kept count of the expenses to feed so many people. It wasn't a small bill, but HaShem had prospered their business in the past year. He sent up a silent prayer of thanksgiving for the referrals they gained from the head servant of Herodium.

Imah looked like a new bride. Her cheeks flushed, and her eyes shone as she stood at Abba's side.

"Where is the precious beauty I keep hearing so much about?" One of the older women nudged Imah's elbow. "It is cruel to invite all of us here only to keep her hidden away."

"Is it not you who always says 'sleep is the best beauty treatment', Jael?" Imah teased. "You wouldn't want me to wake her prematurely."

Jael's shoulders drooped in a dramatic fashion. "Oh, caught in my own advice. Very well, I suppose we will wait. I pray she is as lovely as her mother and as wise as her grandmother."

Abba's eyes sparkled, and he wrapped an arm around Imah's shoulders.

Malon's gaze shifted back to the courtyard gate. Savta was also radiant. Her face lit with pride as she and Aunt

Tzivyah hovered near the gate greeting guests and ushering them inside and toward the dining area.

"All this fuss over a baby who won't even remember it." Uncle Tiltan gave him a playful shove as he snatched a grape from the bowl and popped it into his mouth. "Don't you wish you remembered your own feast, Malon?"

"I don't know. Was the food good?"

His uncle tilted his head to the side and placed a finger on his chin. "I was only about thirteen at the time. I think, Tzivyah burned the fish at your feast. Don't tell her I told you. She'll slay me in my sleep." He gave Malon a jab in the ribs. "Now, if you'll excuse me, my mother insists it is time for me to mingle with the men of the city and arrange a marriage with a suitable match." With a wink, Uncle Tiltan sauntered off.

Malon bustled around the house, checking lamps to ensure they didn't run out of oil, seeing that the wine didn't falter and the food remained piled high upon the plates.

At last, Topaz's wail escalated above the clamor, and all the guests applauded. Abba emerged carrying the babe, and a crowd gathered around. Malon took advantage of the distraction to check the food one last time. The mound of figs hadn't diminished, the *musht* fish still filled half its platter with the artichoke, but the nuts and pomegranate were dwindling. He picked up the dishes and headed for the kitchen.

"Malon, you never rest, do you?" Rabbi Ben-Elior caught his elbow. "Your father will have to hire more servants to keep up with you."

"Shalom, Rabbi. It is good to see you. You haven't been to the shop in some time."

"Yes, I must admit I am surprised your father asked me to be here tonight."

"You have been a good friend of ours for many years."

"True, but your father and I had a bit of a disagreement."

"It's been almost three years since I've seen David."

"He has grown into a fine man." A sparkle lit the rabbi's eye. "He is well learned in the Torah and can recite one hundred of the prophecies of the coming Messiah."

How strange his words seemed. Ben-Elior and his son had been the closest of friends to Malon and his father during his mother's sickness, but now the issue of the Messiah divided them. Knowing all those Scriptures by heart, how could they not see Jesus was indeed the One they had been waiting for?

"Shalom, everyone. Sorry I am late." No mistaking that booming voice. Uncle Noah.

A smile stretched Malon's face. Malon leaned close to

Ben-Elior and whispered, "But he brought gifts."

The rabbi chuckled.

"I may be late," Uncle Noah proclaimed. "But I am not empty handed. Where is that niece of mine? I brought her the finest of all the gifts." The old man pressed through the crowd to stand before Imah. "How beautiful you are yet, my niece. You have not aged a day since I last saw you. What is this? A baby girl? Oh, and she is every bit as lovely as her mother."

Uncle Noah took the babe into his arms and cradled her against his robust bosom.

Abba held up a hand and spoke over the crowd. "Since we have everyone's attention, I would like to thank you all for coming to celebrate this blessing HaShem has sent to our home. As most of you know, our family was torn apart for many years. Aaliyah became infected with the terrible disease of leprosy and was away from us for ten years. But now, the God who restores and provides has united us again as a family. More than that, He has blessed us with another member. Praise HaShem!"

With smiles lining their voices, friends and family echoed his praise.

"At this time, we would like to ask Rabbi Ben-Elior if he would say a blessing over our daughter."

The rabbi blinked, his neck jolting a little. But he

stepped forward and congratulated Abba and Imah. Uncle Noah pouted but surrendered the babe, and the rabbi raised her toward heaven.

"Source of life, You who called the Patriarchs and blessed the Matriarchs, to You we turn now in prayer. May You bless the parents of this newly born daughter to whom they have given the name Topaz. As You were with Abraham, Isaac, and Jacob, Sarah, Rebekah, Rachel, and Leah, may You be with these parents and this new child. Sustain them in life and in health. May the joy of this moment remain. May these parents gain the wisdom, which will enable them to raise their daughter with love and understanding, avoiding the pits of false teachers. May this child grow to maturity secure in Your love and shaped by the love of her parents. May the ancient hope of Torah be realized in her so she may achieve devoted learning, marital bliss, and good deeds. Amen."

"Amen." Abba took Topaz from the rabbi and placed her in Imah's arms. "Thank you, Rabbi. We are honored you would come."

"Mazel tov, Tyrus. As I said, I hope Adonai will grant you the wisdom to raise your children in love and understanding, and help you to avoid the pits of false teachings."

Even from where he stood, Malon recoiled from the

stab of his comment. But Abba handled it with a gracious smile. "He is, my friend. He has blessed me greatly. You see my wife? She is completely whole."

"So I have heard."

"Now you have not just heard, but seen. The teacher from Nazar—"

"Yes, I have heard your claims circulating in the temple. Tyrus, you are my friend. I have two purposes in being here tonight. The first was the blessing of your child, but the second is far more serious. I'm sure you have felt the effect of the priests' business being taken elsewhere."

"I have, but the Lord provides."

Ben-Elior shook his head. "The priests are ready to do far more than ceasing their purchasing from you. If you continue to profess this Jesus, to follow his teachings, they will expel you from the synagogue. If that happens, no faithful Jew in this town will buy from you or even greet you in the street. You will be treated as an infidel. I do not wish for that to happen."

"Neither do I, Rabbi, but how can I deny the man who healed my wife? He told me things about my situation that only God would know. How do you explain that away? He must be the Messiah."

The rabbi's jaw tightened. "You are too stubborn, Ben-Adamiel, but I have warned you. Let this serve as a warning for all of you." Raising his chin with his voice, Ben-Elior addressed the guests. "Anyone who professes Jesus as the Christ, and continues to follow his teachings, will be expelled by the elders as a heretic."

Fury boiled inside Malon. He tipped his head, taking in the guests' horrified faces. Ben-Elior had ruined the occasion and poisoned dozens into rejecting the true Messiah.

What did it matter? Soon the Messiah will make his stand in Jerusalem. Then all will see who he truly is. Any day now.

Chapter Three

"Anger will help nothing, Malon."

The jars inside the crate rattled as Malon shoved them onto the cart. He wheeled around to face his father. "How dare he come to our dedication feast and turn it into…a disaster? I have never heard of anything so rude. The man is a leader in this community, and yet he shows forth such lack of decorum."

"The rabbi is concerned for the welfare of his people."

Malon took a deep breath and leaned against the cart. The rabbi and his family had been their friends for so long. He should be careful how he spoke of him. "It doesn't make sense. Don't the rabbis look for the coming of the Messiah more than we do? Why should they fear him?"

"They do seek the Messiah, but they do not agree with all of Jesus' teachings. He condemns them for their traditions. Simon said — "

"Do you mean Peter?" He gave his father an attempt at a smile. "That's what Jesus calls him."

"I have known him my entire life as Simon. Very well, then." Abba winked. "Peter said Jesus told the scribes and Pharisees they were of their father the devil."

A chuckle bubbled up within Malon, dissipating the remnants of his anger. He imagined horror on the scribes' faces at those words. "I suppose that did not please them."

"No. Jesus says they have a knowledge of the mind, but not of the heart."

"How long must we wait for him to take his rightful place in Jerusalem? When will he assemble the army to extricate the Romans?"

"Patience, my son. God's timing is not our own, but if what Simon..." He held up his hands. "Sorry. *Peter* says is true, we will not have to wait much longer."

Malon settled back and rubbed his itching, scabbed shoulders against the cart's edge. He envisioned children running through the streets without fear of being trampled by Roman cohorts. What would it be like to be free of the talons of the great imperial eagle? The desire to taste such freedom burned in his throat.

"Was that the last crate?" Abba's voice pulled him out of the daydream.

"Oh. Yes, but there was one more sack of grain. I'll fetch it." He jogged into the house, peeking at Imah and the babe as he passed the open door. It had taken all morning to set their house to right after the feast—a small effort in comparison to keeping Imah in bed during it all. He and his father were both determined to make her heal for several more weeks before allowing her to do household chores again. For now, she sat in her chair, Topaz in her arms, her fingertips tracing the sleeping infant's plump cheek and lips.

Something inside Malon's bosom squeezed tight. How many precious moments like this one had been stolen from him? Had he known his mother was alive all those years—leprosy or not—he would have seen her. Even if just to watch from a distance as he did now. That his abba and aunt had hidden her existence from him still stung. He felt like an olive, pressed beneath a heavy weight, the life inside him draining out his eyes.

Imah looked up. The concern in her warm, brown eyes chased away her smile. "Are you all right? Do you need more salve on your back?"

"I'm fine, Imah." He would never tire of that most precious word. "You're just so beautiful."

Pulling himself away, he stepped into the kitchen and swiped the moisture from his cheeks before hefting the sack onto his shoulder. He winced, not from the weight of the sack, but the weight of the regret tugging at his heart. How could a woman so sweet and lovely have lived in a despairing leper colony? She had to have been the only light in that place.

He stood with the sack, while dust danced in the light filtering through the lattice window. If he'd asked more questions, pushed his father more, perhaps she would not have been abandoned so long. He wouldn't have been deprived of a mother during the years he needed her most. Instead, he let the lies of his father and aunt manipulate him.

No matter how he wriggled, he found himself strung up in someone else's control — be it Roman rule, priestly traditions, or tyrannical extortions. All plagued his family. Someone constantly watched their moves and manipulated their options.

Malon choked. The air in the kitchen suddenly felt close. He needed to get back outside. He hurried through the courtyard and shoved his weight against the door to the street. The door gave way, and he stumbled through. The grain sack slipped from his shoulder as he collided with a young woman. Her bronze eyes widened, and she toppled backward onto the cobblestone street, the breath escaping her lips in a small cry.

He shifted his weight and barely caught himself and the sack, before tumbling on top of her. What was she doing at his house? And who was she?

Peter's wife, Hannah, rushed to the girl's side. "Petronilla, are you all right?"

Petronilla? Peter had spoken of his daughter, but for whatever reason, Malon had imagined her younger.

"Malon, do you have to come stampeding through the door?" Hannah chided.

"I'm sorry. I didn't know she was there."

"Mercy, child, anyone could have been on the other side of that door."

Child. Not her too. Hadn't he been called that enough in the last few weeks?

"I'm all right, Imah." Petronilla's face reddened like a blossoming rose, and her gaze dropped behind long dark lashes. "You needn't scold him."

Hannah helped the girl to her feet, and he lobbed the grain sack into the cart. A cloud of dust rose with the thud, giving him a good excuse to clear his throat.

Abba gave Malon a knowing grin. "Before the collision, Hannah was saying that Peter and the Master will be coming here soon."

"They will?" Malon hated the boyish excitement in his voice, but he couldn't help it. Each time he heard Jesus speak, he felt as though life was breathed into him — life and a hope for the future.

Hannah smiled. "Yes, they will be stopping by here before they head to Judea, and then Jerusalem for the Passover Feast."

His heart skipped a beat. The Master was going to Jerusalem. For the Passover Feast. Could it be, Jesus would enter the city of Zion to take his place as the Messiah? "When will they arrive?"

"Tomorrow or the day after, I believe, but they won't stay long. The Master wishes to go by Judea before Passover. Peter sent word asking me to prepare the house. Petronilla and I have been scurrying like conies trying to get everything ready, but we had to take a few moments to visit your mother and the precious new babe. May we go in?"

"Of course." Abba grinned. "Aaliyah will be delighted to see you, but please, make sure she stays in bed. We want her to heal good and proper."

"I'll make sure of it." With a nod, Hannah ushered her daughter inside.

When the door closed behind them, Malon stepped toward the cart. "Shall we get these things to the shop? We've much work to do."

"That we do, and I expect you will want to leave early

tomorrow if Jesus arrives."

"Yes, Abba, if it isn't too much trouble."

"I think if we work a bit faster today, we will both be able to go."

Malon leapt up into the cart and grabbed the reins. "Just think, Abba, Jesus going to Jerusalem for the Passover."

"Many Jews go to Jerusalem for the Passover."

"Yes, but Jesus is the Messiah."

"He has been to Jerusalem for the feast before."

"But it's perfect. Passover is the feast commemorating the time HaShem freed our people from the bondage of Egypt. It must be time. Jesus will enter the city and begin the deliverance. Soon, we will be free from Roman rule."

*****

People crowded Peter's house by the time Malon and his father finished work and arrived at the hut. Rising on his tiptoes, Malon peered over countless heads. "There they are. Peter and Andrew are over there, Abba."

"I see them. Come on."

Following his father, Malon squeezed around men, women, and children toward the two men standing by the door.

"Simon," Abba called, but his friend didn't hear. "Simon…Peter."

Peter's matted head turned, and wisps of wild hair obscured his face. "Tyrus." The fisherman smiled and strode toward them. "I'm glad to see you. How is your wife?"

"She and the babe are both healthy and happy." Abba clasped his friend's arm. "Your wife and daughter are well too, in case you were wondering."

Peter's russet eyebrow quirked. "Don't tease me, my friend. I have missed them terribly. I would take them with me, but…" He offered a shrug.

Malon stepped forward. "But what?"

One of Peter's callused fisherman hands touched a sword at his side. "Well, I am willing to fight to the death beside the Master, but endangering my family is something else. I think it will be soon. The Master has been talking about this journey to Jerusalem, and then…well, and I can't say the rest. I don't know exactly what will happen, but I think soon something will. The chief priests become increasingly hostile. Even more so after the happenings in Bethany."

Abba frowned. "What happened in Bethany?"

"Haven't you heard? Jesus' good friend Lazarus had fallen ill. His sisters sent word to the Master, begging him to come, but he tarried by the Jordan for some days before going to Bethany. By the time we arrived, Lazarus had been dead four days. Jesus stood at the entrance of the tomb and commanded them to roll away the stone."

"After *four* days?"

Malon smiled for the question had come simultaneously from Abba.

"Yes. Lazarus' sister warned him the smell would be bad, but he told her to only believe. So the men rolled away the stone."

Nods encouraged Peter to continue.

"From the tomb emerged a stench worse than rotting fish — so terrible everyone groaned and covered their noses and mouths. All, that is, except the Master. He stepped forward and lifted his eyes to heaven and prayed. Then he called in a loud voice, 'Lazarus, come forth.'"

"He called out to the dead man?" Abba squinted and rubbed his jaw at Peter's tale.

"He did. At first, I didn't know what to think. Sometimes the Master does the strangest things. Then a sound came from the open tomb. All the people stood with eyes transfixed on the opening. We heard shuffling steps. Then Lazarus came out of the tomb."

Abba's mouth fell open, and surely, Malon's expression mirrored his shock. "But...Lazarus had been dead? Truly dead?"

"For four days. No mistaking it. A live person would not have caused such a stench. The man was dead, believe me."

"What did Jesus do then?"

"He commanded us to loose Lazarus of his grave clothes and let him go. The man is alive and well today. We are going to Bethany to visit him before we return to Jerusalem for the Passover."

Abba shook his head. "A miracle like no other. Why does this make you nervous about returning to Jerusalem?"

"I'm more anxious than nervous. Many people saw Lazarus emerge from the tomb. Many believed, but some returned to the priests and reported what happened. The news served to make the priests more wary of Jesus. They call him the Prince of Devils, doing such miracles by the power of Beelzebub. The last time we were in Jerusalem, the crowd became so angry they sought to stone the Master. Now you see why I cannot take my family with me this time. I may be required to wield a sword on Jesus' behalf, but if it brings the liberation faster, then it's what I will do."

Abba arched one brow at Malon as he folded his arms across his chest. "I understand what you mean. We want to keep our family safe."

Running a hand through his tousled hair, Peter nodded. "Tyrus, if something should happen to me—"

"Don't fret, Simon. Your family will be looked after."

The fisherman's eyes glossed over as he clasped Abba's arm. "Thank you." After a long moment, Peter shifted his attention to Malon. "Good to see you, my young friend. Jesus has asked about you."

"He has?"

"Yes, he said he hopes to speak with you while we are here."

Malon peered beyond the disciple at Jesus sitting with a small child on his lap. The child ran his tiny fingers through the Teacher's beard. Malon's pulse quickened in his veins. What would the Master wish to say to *him*?

Peter tipped his head in Jesus' direction. "Go on. Greet him. You won't be interrupting anything. He does not wish to speak to the public during this visit."

Pulse now thundering in his ears, Malon approached the Master. As he drew near, Jesus lifted his eyes to him. The pools of deep blue pierced his soul. "There is my young disciple."

Jesus claimed him as a disciple. His heart soared. "I've yet to follow you, Lord, but it is my desire."

"Even as a true son hears the will of his father and

does it, so a true disciple also follows his master's teachings. In this you have been faithful."

"Yes, Rabbi, but my heart calls me to walk after you."

"You hear my Father's call, Malon. He will use you, and your youth, for His glory. One day you will go where I lead you, but this is not that day." The boy in the Master's lap wiggled, and Jesus stroked the child's unruly, black curls with a smile. "How is your family?"

"My mother and sister are both well. My father is here." Malon pointed to Abba talking with Peter.

The Master's grin widened. "The Lord delights when a family dwells together in unity. It is His masterpiece."

"His blessings are upon us."

"Have patience, Malon. In the Lord's time, your father will release you. Then follow me with all your heart and all your might."

He blinked. The Master was calling him. A simple merchant's son from a fishing town in Judea. Yet Jesus, the Messiah, was calling *him*. A slight breeze from the Galilee would have been enough to send him sprawling to the floor. When at last he found his voice, "Yes, Lord," was all he could say.

The Teacher shifted to Peter as he and Abba approached Malon's side. "What do you think, Peter? Do kings of the earth collect their taxes from their own children, or from strangers?"

The fisherman's brows knitted together. "From strangers."

"So then, the children are exempt." The Master shrugged. "Nevertheless, so that we don't offend them, go to the sea, cast a hook, and the first fish that you catch, look in his mouth. You will find money. Take it, and use it to pay the tribute for both of us."

Malon studied Peter's face. His eyes were wide as the Galilee, and he stood still as the cliffs surrounding it. He would have to ask him more about it later.

Jesus shifted the boy in his arms and stood. He beckoned to his disciples. "Phillip, James, John, my children, come to me."

Malon stepped back to make room for the twelve as they gathered around the Master, waiting for him to speak.

"Tell me, what is it you argued about on the journey?"

Peter looked at Andrew, who looked at James and John. No one answered.

With a sigh, Jesus sat again. "If any of you wish to be the greatest of all, you must first be the servant of all." He extended a hand to the child before him. "Unless you humble yourselves and become as one of these little children, you will not enter the kingdom of heaven."

The boy took Jesus' hand and crawled onto his lap once again.

"Whoever receives one of these little children in my name, the same receives me, and whoever does not receive me, does not refuse me, but the One that sent me."

Malon listened intently as the Master spoke, but many of the sayings confused him. How he wished he could walk by the way with him, ask him questions, and hear all he had to say. Maybe then he would understand, as Jesus' disciples seemed to.

After some time, Peter rose and left the room. Malon glanced at Abba, who gave him a nod, so he followed.

"Peter, wait." He jogged to catch up with the disciple's long strides. "Where are you going?"

The fisherman held up a line and hook. "To catch a fish. Would you like to accompany me?"

Malon's grin was answer enough, and he fell into step beside Peter. "I wanted to ask you about that. You seemed shocked when the Master asked your opinion of the tribute, but it is that time of year. Why would it be strange for him to question you about it?"

"Just today, as we were entering the city, the tax collectors asked me if my Master paid tribute. I didn't know what else to say, so I said yes. I had meant to ask Jesus about it, but I had yet to do so when he broached the subject."

"Do you think he overheard your conversation?"

"It isn't likely. He was engaged in a discussion with the Pharisees."

"How puzzling."

"Things like this happen all the time. This is the sign my father, Zebedee, taught me to look for in the Messiah. He knows the secrets of the hearts. The Father shows him all things."

When they reached the seashore, the other fishermen were preparing for the night's catch. Peter selected one of their small boats and readied the line while Malon swiped at cobwebs and ants residing in the unused boat.

"Are you fishing with a hook?" Malon asked.

"I only need to catch one fish. Besides, the Master said to 'cast in my hook'. If there's one thing I've learned while walking with Jesus these past few years, it is that you must do all things exactly as he said."

They climbed into the boat and launched onto the Galilee. They rowed a few paces, and then sat still. Peter baited his hook, and then cast his line into the sea. Soon, a jerk tugged at the other end.

Peter's skilled hands reeled the line in. "This is it. Just as the Master said." He withdrew the hook from the fish's mouth and handed it to Malon. "Hold this so I can look inside."

His thick fingers pried at the fish's mouth. "I can see something, but my fingers are not nimble enough to retrieve it. Here, yours are smaller. You try."

Peter clasped the wiggling fish in both hands, and Malon stuck his finger inside the sticky mouth. The fading light of sunset made it difficult to see past the sharp little teeth pricking his skin. His fingernail brushed against something, and he pinched it between his fingers. Straining to extract it without losing his grasp, he twisted it and tugged it free. He gasped as he recognized the round object. "Just as Jesus said."

"Yes, the piece is enough for his tribute and mine." The fisherman jostled the fish in his hand. "How did *you* come upon such a treasure, eh, little fish?"

The fish squirmed in response, and Peter tossed it into the sea. He placed the coin in his pouch and sat down at the oars.

Malon took hold of an oar and pulled hard. Rowing looked easy when watching from shore. Little wonder his companion had callused hands and arms like a cedar. A scab on Malon's back tore open, and he paused, allowing the pain to dull. "Peter, you said you suspect something to happen when you reach Jerusalem."

The fisherman squinted from under his thick brows.

"You wish to go with us, don't you?"

"More than anything."

"A few days ago, Jesus mentioned danger when we go to Jerusalem. Judging by his various remarks, I think it may be time to begin the conquest. It will be perilous, but a time unlike any other in history. You're a man now. If you and your father wish to come, you are welcome to do so. I'm sure Jesus would be glad to have you along. Our numbers diminished a few weeks ago when many of his followers left, so any extra swords would make me feel much better. Should you choose to go, you will be witnessing the greatest time in all of history."

Chapter Four

"Then Peter invited us to join him." Malon held his breath and waited for his father's reply.

The chair screeched under Abba when he stood up from behind the desk. He picked up the logs and avoided Malon's gaze as he crossed the shop floor and put them away. "I can't go to Jerusalem now. I have your mother, sister, and the shop to look after. We have another caravan departing to Herodium this week."

"Then please, at least allow me to go. I will be with Peter and Andrew. And with Jesus."

"I know. That is what worries me."

"I want to enter Jerusalem with Jesus. I want to see him bring the deliverance."

"What do you think that means, Malon? Do you think he will walk to the temple mount, proclaim himself the

Messiah, and every priest and Roman will bow to him? Crown him as king?" Abba crossed his arms over his chest. "No. The priests all hate him. They call him the Prince of Devils, and the Romans are no better. There's bound to be violence. How many will die?"

Malon stepped backward. "But Jesus works miracles."

"You think his miracles will make an entire empire hand over one of the most coveted cities in the world? Tell me, how will Jesus bring this deliverance?"

Something sunk like a stone in his gut. His father was right. He hadn't thought of what deliverance would entail. Malon bit his lip and plopped onto a barrel. He wanted to go. But the set of Abba's jaw gave him little hope. "You have trained me with a sword."

"To protect caravans against bandits, not to battle trained soldiers." Abba let out a heavy sigh and ran a hand through his dark tresses. "We've only begun to be a family again. Are you not content to live as a happy family with your mother and baby sister? All I had lost has only begun to be restored. Can you blame me for wishing to keep it for as long as possible?"

"The culmination of all the prophecies travels to Jerusalem. Once in all of time will the promised Messiah take his stand in the city."

Abba placed a hand on Malon's shoulder. "I can't let

you go. If anything happened to you…" His breath came in jagged puffs. "I just can't. Tarry with me awhile longer. You will have your chance to serve the Messiah, but not yet. You heard what Simon said. There is danger on every side. The priests seek to kill Jesus. This will be the work of zealots, not of tradesmen like us."

"Zealots. Is that what you consider Jesus and Peter to be?" Malon measured his tone. Despite the passion rising in him, he was speaking to his father.

"Jesus is a man of peace, but that may have to change. Sometimes war is necessary, but I am not ready to let you go."

A familiar feeling spread through his chest. The same feeling that haunted him the day he found out his mother was alive. *This is different. At least he's being honest with you.* Still, it felt the same. He was controlling him. Keeping him from what he believed was the right thing.

Have patience.

That is what Jesus had said. So then, that is what he would do.

*****

Malon coughed as the dust from the camel train settled into every crevice in the marketplace. Kish brought the train to a halt. Abba's former apprentice was already gaining ownership in the trade and handled most of the business in the outlying villages, as well as the imports from Caesarea.

"This journey seems to lengthen each time." Kish jumped from his beast and brushed sand off his tunic. When Malon held out a cup of water, Kish accepted it with a smile. "I hope our profits make it worth it."

"You hope? You'd better know." Abba emerged from the shop. "Where are the logs?"

Kish's signature grin showed his big teeth as it spread across his tanned face. He retrieved the scrolls from the camel's pack. Abba accepted them and gave him a skeptical quirk of the brow before disappearing inside the shop.

Malon couldn't help but laugh. Since Kish excelled to partner, he and Abba formed a very interesting bond.

"How is Jerusalem?" Malon asked as he stepped over to unload the camels.

"Clamorous. It's busy as ever, but about to shred in two over the Nazarene healer. As we were leaving, Jesus entered the city. He was riding a donkey, and the people were waving palm branches as if he were a king, ready to claim his throne. Many people threw their cloaks on the ground for the donkey to trod upon. 'Hosanna to the Son of David' they shouted. I thought the entire garrison of soldiers might show up and arrest him at such a proclamation, but they didn't. I suppose there were too many people." Kish shook his head, specks of sand flinging as he did. "Amazing how a mob can rule. The children sang songs of praise saying, 'Blessed is he who comes in the name of the Lord.' I glimpsed the priests as I left the city. Could have smoldered a log with the intensity of their glares."

"Is Jesus safe? Did he enter the city in peace?"

"Yes, as far as I could tell. Of course, who knows what happened after I left."

Malon's stomach fluttered. The Messiah had entered Jerusalem, as a king, in peace. The people had accepted him, and the priests and the Romans could do nothing about it. Kish never offered opinions on the matter, but one thing was certain, this was the day Israel had been waiting for. Whether they knew it or not.

Malon turned his gaze toward Jerusalem. "If only I'd been there."

"Been where? Jerusalem? Trust me, it's not where you want to be. It's too crowded this time of year. It seems all Israel is gathering for the Passover feast."

"Everyone—except me."

Kish leveled his gaze at Malon as he hoisted a crate

onto his shoulder. "That city is no place for a lad of your age. True, the city holds the temple, but it also holds all manner of evils. Thieves, prostitutes, Roman soldiers — I believe the devil himself may be lurking in that city. Stay where you belong and be glad about it."

Malon fisted his hands at his sides as he bit back a retort to the lad-of-his-age comment. He shouldered a load and worked in silence.

Abba soon joined them, and it didn't take long to unload the caravan, restock the shelves, and stable the livestock for the night.

When they'd finished reviewing the logs, Abba clasped Kish on the shoulder. "Well done. We made a nice profit on the goods you sold. And you cut a fair deal with our suppliers in Jerusalem, so we're sure to profit from what you brought back as well. We'll finish closing up shop, and you go on home to your wife and child."

Though Kish was a full-grown man, he never failed to beam with any praise Abba bestowed. "Thank you, sir. I think I'll do just that. It's been a long journey, and I'm anxious to see them."

After Kish left the shop, Malon paused before the open window as the sun sank behind the Galilee. "Abba, Jesus entered Jerusalem as Kish was leaving town."

Abba's quill ceased its scratching. "Did he?"

"Yes, the people hailed him as a king. He rode into the city upon a donkey, and they strew their coats on the road for him. There was nothing the priests or even the Romans could do. He has entered in peace."

"Upon a donkey?"

Malon glanced at him over his shoulder. "That's what Kish said."

Abba's eyes squinted. "It seems there was a prophecy concerning the Messiah and a donkey. Hurry and close the shop, we'll go to the synagogue and find out. I can finish these logs tomorrow."

Without giving Abba time for hesitation, Malon obeyed. The night was warm, and the first stars winked from the sky as the last hints of daylight slipped behind the Galilee. They mounted the white limestone steps and entered the temple under carvings of vines and pomegranates signifying the beauty of Jehovah. Two priests were lighting the lamps inside the synagogue. When they saw Malon and Abba, a look of disgust lifted one side of the taller one's mouth, and they turned their backs. Malon had seen similar reactions when harlots passed them on the streets. Abba tensed, but it didn't bother Malon. If the priests and scribes wanted to spurn the truth, that was their business.

The rabbis standing nearby cast disapproving stares as

they approached the cabinet containing the sacred Torah and books of prophecy. One stepped toward them, and Malon wondered if he would prevent them from approaching, but another caught his arm. "You've no cause to keep them from the books. Perhaps they will see the light of truth as they read."

Though stilled by his companion's words, the priest glowered as Abba and Malon lifted their tallits to cover their heads and sat before the ark.

"The book of the prophecy of Zechariah, please," Abba whispered to the minister. The man arched one brow, but selected the scroll and handed to him, watching them with the eyes of a hawk.

Abba plucked it up and gently unrolled the parchment, his dark eyes scanning the lines of Hebrew letters. "Here it is. 'Rejoice greatly, O daughter of Zion; shout, O daughter of Jerusalem; behold thy King cometh unto thee; he is just, and having salvation; lowly, and riding upon a donkey, and upon a colt the foal of a donkey.'"

"Amazing. May I see it?" Malon reached out and grasped the book from Abba. He stared at the prophecy. "Look, it continues, 'And I will cut off the chariot from Ephraim, and the horse from Jerusalem, and the battle bow shall be cut off; and he shall speak peace unto the heathen; and his dominion shall be from sea even to sea, and from the river even to the ends of the earth.'" He caught Abba's gaze. "See, Abba, he comes in peace. The battle bow is broken. If this first half of the prophecy is fulfilled, the second will be as well. There will be no fighting."

"You say this because you want to join Jesus in Jerusalem."

"Do you not wish to see prophecy fulfilled before your very eyes? Surely, you are still young enough to understand the craving in my soul."

Abba reclaimed the scroll and rolled it up. Returning it to the minister, he stood and led Malon toward the exit. "I understand, my son. I suppose I have been selfish in not allowing you to go. If Jesus has entered the city in peace, then I see no harm in you joining him."

Malon could have leapt as high as the moon shining above the outer court. "Will you really permit me to go?"

"We will be sending another caravan to Jerusalem at the end of the week. I advise you to take time to pray about the matter. Then, if you still wish to go, you may ride with it to the city."

He threw his arms around his father's shoulders, whose form stiffened in his forceful embrace. "Thank you."

"Crushing me is no way to thank me." His father gave

a small cough.

Malon pulled back, unable to suppress the stupid grin he knew tugged at his lips. "I will help the Messiah in whatever way I can. I will make you proud."

Abba's eyes glossed over, and he touched Malon's shoulder. "I am already proud, my son. Go, and live the adventure you've always dreamed of."

Chapter Five

The midday sun glinted off Jerusalem's magnificent marble gate. The soft tinkle of the lead camel's bells lost to the clamor around them as they entered.

Malon's heart all but leapt out of his chest. With the setting of the sun, Shabbat would begin, and he would be free to follow the Messiah day and night. Soon he would actually see Jesus at his rightful place in the temple.

The splendor and busyness of Jerusalem always stunned him from the moment the arched gates came into sight. The market. The temple. The people from around the world, all mingling in the streets. Every bit of it captivating.

The camels plodded along the cobblestones as his gaze flitted about. Everything seemed as it usually was. No excitement, no celebration, only people going about their everyday life. Strange. He'd expected to enter a city alive with anticipation, but he observed the opposite.

They halted the camel train before the Cardo market. Circular pavilions with the typical roman style columns held merchant booths containing every item one could imagine. Scents of spices, nuts, dye and animals wafted through the air. People bustled about in red, blue, and purple tunics, each intent on completing the week's tasks and purchasing what goods were needed in time for the Sabbath.

Malon and Kish arranged the most attractive goods beneath the canopy and secured the rest beneath canvas to prevent theft. They finished as the sun was sinking behind the city wall.

"It's too late to go to the temple tonight." Kish shrugged. "So I suppose you'll have to stay with me at my uncle's house."

Malon hesitated. Why did he get the feeling that it was more disappointing to Kish than it was to him? The apprentice usually enjoyed having Malon along. At least, so he said.

"Unless you want to rent a place in the merchant quarters." Kish amended.

"I don't mind staying with you. The merchant quarters can't rival your aunt's cooking."

"Promise me one thing, Malon." Kish paused as they exited the market. "Don't mention to my uncle that you will become a disciple of Jesus."

"And if he asks me of my plans?"

"Just tell him you are zealous to serve the Lord. He won't think it odd that you go to the temple on the Sabbath, so it shouldn't be a problem as long as you hold your tongue."

How weary he grew of the divisions between the Jews. Nevertheless, he nodded. He needed somewhere to sleep tonight, and he would honor Kish's request for that reason.

*****

Malon rose and stretched. How nice to do so without pain reminding him of Gallus. Faint light glowed through the window and provided help as he fumbled to gather his belongings. When he made his way toward the door, he kicked a bucket, and it clattered across the room.

Kish raised his head from his blanket. "Do you intend to wake the entire house?"

"I'm sorry," Malon whispered. "I didn't want to light a lamp, but I've defeated my own purpose."

The corners of the apprentice's mouth dipped. "Off

you go then."

Malon dusted his hands on his tunic. He wasn't sure why Kish acted so stiff. Maybe because, come the first of the week, it would leave him to do all the work. "I'll send messages as oft as I can."

He extended a hand. Kish sat up and gave it a firm squeeze. "God be with you."

"I know He will be." How could God be any closer than when one walked beside the Messiah? He lifted the latch and exited the house as quietly as he could.

He inhaled deeply, the morning air penetrating his lungs and awakening his senses. With quick steps, he strode toward the temple mount. Passing a garrison of Roman soldiers, he wondered how much longer Jesus would tolerate their presence. Perhaps he was working even now to remove them. Wouldn't that be marvelous? He could hardly imagine an Israel without Romans controlling their every move.

He mounted the temple stairs two at a time. The low tones of the Levitical Choir soothed his ears. But…Where were all the people? Throngs of thousands usually followed Jesus everywhere. Even when he sailed across the Galilee to other parts of the country, they followed him. Malon wandered about Solomon's Porch. Torches hung from the walls. Tall marble columns cast shadows across his path as he meandered through the faithful Shabbat gatherers. But no sign of Jesus or his disciples.

He approached the gate called Beautiful, and a beggar tugged on his tunic. "Please, sir, alms for a lame brother?"

Malon extracted a coin from his purse and dropped it into the man's hand. "Do you know where the teacher from Nazareth is?"

"You mean Jesus?"

"Yes, Jesus of Nazareth."

"Where have you been, boy? Everyone knows where he is."

No need to respond to the belittling comment. "I've recently arrived. Where is he?"

"In the garden."

"Which garden? Gethsemane?"

"No, lad, the garden of tombs."

"Tombs? I don't understand. Please speak plainly, sir."

The beggar sighed and shifted his weight from one tattered side to the other. "He's dead. They've buried him in a tomb."

The words sucked the breath from Malon's lungs. "No, it can't be. He is the one who entered the city several days ago on a donkey."

"Yes," the beggar snorted. "The mob changes its mind quick, doesn't it? One day they hail him as a king, the next cry for crucifixion."

No. Malon cringed. Romans had a way with torture, and crucifixion was their worst. Surely, Jesus could not have fallen to that fate. "You must be confused. Do you know where I can find Jesus' disciples?"

"Nobody knows. They've gone into hiding since Jesus was arrested."

Taking a few steps back, Malon shook his head. This beggar couldn't know anything about what he was speaking of. He must be deluded. Jesus entered the city as the Messiah only days ago. There was no possible way they'd killed him. And even less chance that Peter, Andrew, and the others were hiding out. Peter had purchased a sword, and he'd been ready for a fight. He never would have let anyone take Jesus.

"Either you're a liar or you're misinformed."

The beggar's face turned crimson. "You dare call me a liar, boy? I'll teach you a lesson." He grasped his hobble stick and swung it at Malon. "Take that, you fool."

Scarcely dodging the blow, Malon stumbled backward and fell against the cold, tile floor. Pain seared up his spine and into his head.

"What's going on here?" A scribe appeared, his garments rustling as he scurried toward them.

"The boy has been asking about Jesus of Nazareth. He

called me a liar." The beggar fumed.

A scowl transformed the scribe's face as he looked down his sharp nose at Malon. "Are you one of Jesus' disciples?"

"If he were one of Jesus' disciples," the beggar's mocking tone grated, "he'd know what happened to his master and be hiding out with the rest. And he certainly wouldn't be calling me a liar."

"Then you came here seeking Jesus of Nazareth?"

Better to remain silent, lest he anger someone worse than the beggar. Malon nodded.

"Yet you don't know what's happened?"

"I know nothing. I come from Galilee."

"Ah, a fellow Galilean. Well then, allow me to save you time and expense. The beggar tells the truth. Jesus of Nazareth is dead. He was executed for blasphemy. You are blessed by Jehovah to have been spared becoming the disciple of a false prophet. You are but a youth, but I advise you to be much more careful in future." The scribe waved Malon away with his hand. "Now go home where you belong before you get yourself into mischief."

Malon picked himself up off the tile floor and slipped out from under the beggar's glare. He fumbled back to the marketplace. His legs and mind numb either from the blow or from shock. He couldn't tell which.

How could Jesus be dead? Peter hiding? It couldn't be true, but why would the scribe and the beggar lie? Much less carry the same tale?

People bumped and shoved him as he stood in the midst of the marketplace, trying in vain to sort out his surroundings. Where had Kish gone? Which corner had they set up in? He'd been here a dozen times before, but for the first time, he felt utterly lost.

If Jesus was dead, then he'd been wrong. Jesus couldn't be the Messiah, for the Messiah was to bring deliverance to Israel. Yet Jesus had fulfilled so many of the prophecies. Could he have been a mere imposter all this time? No, the miracles he performed were greater than anything Israel had ever known. It must be a lie.

Wait…Jesus had raised a man of Bethany from the dead. Perhaps he had come off the cross alive and was recovering somewhere in the city. Yes, that would make sense as to why his disciples were not appearing in public. He had to find someone who knew where they were.

A young boy skipped past, and Malon stretched out a hand and caught him by the arm. "Boy, do you know Jesus of Nazareth?"

The lad shrugged, jostling a mop of brown hair. "Everyone in Jerusalem knows him."

"Do you know where he is?"

"*Ken*, I know."

"Will you take me to him?"

The boy's face contorted. "I don't know.... There's soldiers."

So Jesus was alive, and he'd been taken by soldiers. Malon reached into his coin purse and held a dinar before the boy's nose. "Take me there, and this will be yours."

The boy's eyes widened. He nodded and waved a hand. "This way."

Malon followed the lad out of the city, and up a hill not far outside the walls. He froze when the boy entered a garden.

"Aren't you coming?" the boy asked.

"What is this place?"

"It's the garden of Joseph of Arimathaea."

With reluctance, Malon followed. There was something eerie about this place....

"Around that corner." The lad pointed a stout finger. "I won't go closer because of the soldiers." Then he held out his hand for the dinar.

Malon took a few steps forward and peered around the grapevines, shrubs, and flowers. A plumed helmet protruded above the leaves.

"Thanks, lad." He dropped the dinar into the boy's waiting palm.

"Can you find your way back?"

"*Ken*. You can run along now."

The boy shrugged, but didn't wait for Malon to change his mind. The boy scampered down the stone path, murmuring his thanks.

After watching him go, Malon turned toward the soldiers. He drew in a deep breath and strode around the corner.

The moment the Romans sighted him, they snapped to attention. "Halt. Who goes there?"

"I am looking for Jesus of Nazareth. Is he here?"

The soldiers looked at each other, then Malon. His pulse quickened as they lifted their spears to a ready position.

The stout one snorted. His eyes pinned Malon. "We're here to guard him, so he'd better be. What is it you want?"

"Where is he? I wish to see him."

"The tomb is sealed. A stone is rolled over the door. No one is allowed in. You may mourn before the sepulcher if you wish, but you cannot see his body."

Malon's shoulders felt heavy. "His body…so he is dead, as the beggar said."

"I don't know anything about a beggar, but he's dead all right. Crucified him yesterday. His was worse than any I've ever seen. Hardly looked like a man after they were through with him."

These words lanced his heart. Jesus had been a man of peace. He'd wrought miracles in their land, healed Malon's mother and restored their family, and they'd given him a cruel and painful death. "What happened?"

"The Jewish Authorities brought Jesus to Pilate and told him they wanted him crucified. Pilate didn't like the idea, so he sentenced him to lashes. After the whipping, they brought him before the crowd, and even as bad as he looked, they still cried out for death. Still of a mind to let Jesus go, the governor offered two criminals to them for his customary release, a nasty man called Barabbas, or Jesus. The stupid mob called for the release of Barabbas rather than this man."

He jolted at the mention of Barabbas's name. "They let Barabbas go?"

"Had to. He was the choice of the crowd. I wasn't happy about it. Neither was anyone else. We worked for a long time to catch that crazy outlaw. After that, the mob grew riotous, and Pilate feared an uprising so, finally, he gave them what they wanted."

He blinked several times to clear his blurred vision. Jesus was dead. Not only that, but Barabbas was on the rampage again. His family had a long and violent history with the outlaw. Would Barabbas target Abba and their family again? What if he did something to Imah and Topaz?

He had to find Peter. Then Barabbas.

Chapter Six

Malon plopped onto the edge of the well and crossed his arms. The passing forms of strangers were becoming more and more shady as daylight faded, and no sign of Peter. After spending the night in the uncomfortable merchant quarters, he was ready to forget the idea of finding him and go home. He must reach his family before Barabbas did.

Still, he needed to speak with Peter. Jesus had shown all the signs of being the Messiah. He couldn't simply die without fulfilling his purpose. There must be something…something everyone had missed, and Peter was his only key.

A splashing kerplop was followed by a cold wave of water on his back. Malon whirled around as a woman drew water from the well. She'd soaked his tunic when she tossed her bucket in. Rather thoughtless of her. Why, if she hadn't been his elder, he would have —

Wait. He knew the woman. He'd seen her when Jesus visited Capernaum. She was also one of his disciples. Her eyes met his for a brief moment before she scurried away.

"Wait. Excuse me, lady."

The woman glanced back. Fear contorted her face, and she picked up her pace.

"Please, woman, I've seen you before. You've been with Jesus." He trotted after her, trying not to lose her form in the crowded streets. She turned down an alley. "Please, I'm a friend of Peter's. I need to find him."

At the mention of Peter, she slowed, and then stopped. Turning around, she squinted at him. "Who are you?"

"I am Malon Ben-Tyrus from Capernaum. Peter is an old family friend. Jesus healed my mother."

"What is it you want?"

"I arrived in Jerusalem last night. I was looking for Jesus, but they tell me he's been executed. I must speak with Peter."

The woman sighed and shifted her water pot to her hip. "Are you alone?"

"Yes."

"Very well then. I will take you to him. Follow me." After another careful glance around the alleyway, the woman continued at a quick pace. Malon followed as they wove in and out of the back streets, and finally up a flight of stairs to an upper chamber.

She gave five raps, and the wooden door opened a crack. "It's me, but I've brought a young man seeking Peter. Says he's an old friend."

The door creaked, and an older woman with a sharp nose poked her head out. She surveyed him in the dim light of her lamp. "What's your name, son?"

"Malon Ben-Tyrus. My father is an old friend of Peter's."

The older woman's lips pursed. She opened the door and motioned the other woman inside. "Come in, Joanna. We're almost ready to visit the tomb. As for you," she turned her calculating eyes on him, "wait here."

The door shut.

Clasping his hands behind his back, he waited for long moments before the door creaked again. "Peter said you may come in."

The old woman ushered him inside and shut the door tightly behind him. "I apologize for the secrecy, but with everything that's happened, we can't be too careful. This way."

He followed her to a well-furnished inner chamber with high cedar ceilings. A long table dominated the room's center, and the disciples gathered around it, although it was too late for a meal.

Peter sat at the end, speaking with another disciple. He looked up as Malon approached, and the emptiness in his eyes stole Malon's breath. "Ah, so your father at last allowed you to come. I'm sorry, son, but you're too late."

"Tell me what you mean, Peter. A few days ago, Kish brought word that Jesus entered Jerusalem, hailed as a king, and went up to the temple in peace. But when I arrive, he has been crucified as a blasphemer? None of this makes sense. What are you doing here? Everyone in Jerusalem says you're in hiding."

"Slow down, Malon. I can hardly understand you." Peter patted the place next to him. "Sit down."

Heaving a sigh, Malon obeyed. "Forgive me, but my head is spinning in every direction, and I can't make sense out of anything."

"We all feel the same way," the disciple opposite Peter said. "You see, Simon? We're not the only ones baffled by what has taken place."

Peter buried his head in his hands. "Do not look to me for answers. I have none to give. I'm as confused as you are."

Malon frowned as he stared at the disciple. Was this the same Simon Peter he'd seen only days before in

Capernaum? The man who was willing to fight to the death for this Jesus of Nazareth, who he swore was the Messiah that was to come? Now, he sat there with the same matted hair, the same fisherman's build, but the fire had gone out of his eyes and his frame stooped.

"Peter, what has happened here?"

After rubbing his weary eyes, the disciple answered, "Jesus did enter Jerusalem, and truly it seemed the people hailed him as a king. Then one of our own, Judas, betrayed him in the garden of Gethsemane, and the soldiers took him away. I tried to fight, but Jesus rebuked me. 'Those who live by the sword will die by the sword,' he said. What else was I to do? I followed at a distance, but could do nothing as they staged a mockery of a trial."

"Did you speak up? You might have testified of his miracles."

"No." Peter bowed his head, his reply hardly audible.

"What did you do then?"

"Nothing."

Malon's brows lowered. "What?"

The fisherman's callused hands clawed at his russet hair. "No. Worse than nothing. I denied him."

If Malon had been standing, he would have taken several steps backward. Or fainted. Instead, splinters stabbed his fingers as he gripped the rough table.

"You…*denied* him?"

"Thrice. I even swore I didn't know him. Don't you see? This is why you should not come to me. I don't have the answers, and I am not fit to lead."

Andrew leaned across the table and touched his brother's arm. "Simon, Jesus called you Peter. A rock. He said he would give you the keys of heaven. If you do not lead us, who will?"

Dropping his hands from his face, Peter looked Andrew in the eye. "I don't know, but it will not be me." He stood up and backed from the table. "I am returning to Galilee. The nets call to Simon the fisherman."

"You are no longer Simon the fisherman, brother. You are Peter, a disciple of Jesus the Christ."

"The Christ? Do you mean the man lying in the tomb outside the city walls? How can I be a disciple to a dead man?"

"The priests are Moses' disciples, and he's been dead for hundreds of years."

"Look where it has gotten them. They are as dead as the man they follow. I refuse to do so."

Malon stared at the brothers as he tried to sort his thoughts. Peter had a point. He didn't want to follow a dead Messiah either. If Jesus really was the Christ, how could he have been killed without completing his purpose? But the miracles Jesus accomplished were too great to be dismissed.

"I remember the first time I met Jesus. He was unlike any man I've ever seen." Andrew's voice quivered. "Do you remember when he turned water to wine at the wedding?"

"Of course, it was the first miracle we witnessed. We saw so many after that, but despite all we saw, some of my favorite moments were when Jesus went fishing with us." A slight smile curved Peter's face, even as tears flowed down his cheeks, glistening on his beard. "Remember when he told the story of Jonah by mouthing the words through one of the fish we caught?"

Grief-filled chuckles rippled through the room.

"He was a good storyteller, and he knew the Torah better than any priest I've heard," one of the sons of Zebedee said. "With no formal teaching, how could Jesus have known so much if he had not been sent of God?"

Peter's eyes flashed. "He was sent of God. No one can deny it. Just because he's dead does not mean he was not sent of God."

"Then what does it mean?" Malon sprung to his feet and looked from one disciple to the other. "Do you believe him to be the Messiah, or don't you? Simon, a few days ago you were willing to die for Jesus and his cause, now you are hiding like a rat in a hole. What has happened to you?"

Peter bowed his head again and swiped at his eyes. "They have killed the Master. I hardly know who I am without him."

The sight of the rough fisherman with tears of mourning dampening his face tempered Malon's fury. How Jesus' disciples loved him. Everyone who truly knew him had loved him. Jesus had done so many good deeds among the people. How could they have killed him? "Is this what Jesus would have you do, then? Hide away in grief forever?"

"We're not going to hide forever, only until the danger dies out."

"You mean until his message dies out. Would he not have you to carry on? To continue in what he preached?"

Peter seated himself at the table again. "What would we preach, Malon? John said Jesus was the one who would come to restore all things. Jesus said he was the door, he was the way, the truth, and the life. How do we preach that with him dead?" He rested his balled fists on the table as he leaned forward, his fiery eyes penetrating Malon's. "Besides, if we as much as show our face in this city, we are liable to be arrested and put to the same death. What would we accomplish?"

"Then what am I to do? I came here to become a disciple of Jesus. I came because I felt God calling me to join this cause."

The sparks in Peter's eyes died out again, and he sat back. "I have no answer for you. What you do is your choice. As for me, I wait here."

Chapter Seven

Any other day, the sunrise over the Galilee would have thrilled Malon to the core. Such a sunrise always seemed to symbolize new opportunities and adventure beyond these hills. Today, annoyance arose at the hint of these possibilities. In Jerusalem he'd found his hopes and aspirations crushed. Jesus failed him. Peter failed him. And here he stood in this fishy town in a stuffy merchant shop. He kicked at a pebble, which ricocheted off the wooden shop door and back at his shin. Growling, he threw his weight against the door, and it flew open, nearly toppling him to the ground with the excess momentum. Why was it unlatched?

"Well, well, the sniffling little boy has grown since I last saw him."

The hair on his neck rose. Only one vagrant in the

country possessed a tone so chilling. His blood pumped in icy bursts. He feared this day, yet prayed and hoped against it. In vain. Again.

He scanned the shop's dim interior, but didn't risk turning to face Barabbas with all his violent extortion. "I heard you'd been released."

"Yes, the people demanded my freedom. You didn't think you could keep me away forever, did you?"

A rough hand gripped the back of Malon's neck, the pressure forcing him to his knees. Barabbas's foul breath surged over him. "Surely, you aren't so naive as to think Barabbas, the Zealot King, would allow you to get away with a dirty little trick like you pulled."

Despite the pounding of his heart, and the urge to fight against the outlaw's grasp, Malon's voice remained steady. "I pulled no tricks, Barabbas. The Romans had been hunting you for months after the insurrection. If you hadn't been in my home, I would have let you be."

Barabbas's grip tightened, his nails digging into Malon's skin. "Bold words for a man so young. Well, your little Roman friends aren't here to help you today."

A cry escaped Malon's lips, his efforts failing to hold back against the pain searing down his spine. *Adonai, help me.* Each nerve tingled in panic. His mind replayed images from his last encounter with Barabbas. He'd spent weeks recovering from the beating, and every inch of his body remembered. His limbs quivered beneath the paralyzing grip on his neck.

"I should squash you like the annoying insect you are. Instead, I've decided to be merciful. Blame it on my good mood in light of being set free." He shoved Malon into a shelf. Clay pots, wooden containers, and baskets rattled and crashed down on top of Malon. Then Barabbas's pinned Malon's chest to the cold floor, the broken shards of pottery gouging through his tunic. The scent of spikenard overpowered him. "Listen close, scum. You have a lovely mother and sister at home, and I'd hate to have to hurt them. You tell your father I will be back at the next silent moon. If you want to keep your family alive and your home from charred ash, you will have six hundred dinars waiting for me on that table." His filthy stub of a finger pointed at Abba's writing desk piled high with scrolls and logs. A low laugh emanated from his chest, and vile mirth burned from his eyes. "The Romans have no charges to arrest me on now, so you've no one to turn to. Seeing you rummage for money with no one to tattle to will give me more enjoyment than killing you."

Barabbas spun to the door, but then stopped. "Oh, and if you fail, as I think you will, it will be most entertaining to hear your mother and sister shriek in fear as I rend them to pieces. Have a good day, scum."

*****

Malon was still shaking uncontrollably when Abba entered. One glance at him and the broken pottery on the floor, and Abba's face paled. "What's happened? Are you ill?"

His father's long strides closed the gap between them, and a protective hand tilted his head. "You have blotches on your neck, and you're pale as death. What has happened to you?"

"Barabbas is free."

"Barabbas." Abba stumbled backward over debris strewn across the floor and bumped into a shelf. "Free? How?"

"Pilate released him during the Passover feast. The crowd chose to free Barabbas and crucify Jesus."

"It can't be true."

"The marks you spoke of on my neck do not lie, Abba."

"Are you certain it was him?"

"I could not see his face, because he attacked me from behind. But I could no more mistake his voice, or the reek of his breath, than I could mistake Jesus."

Abba winced. "What does he want?"

"Six hundred dinars before the next silent moon, or he will harm Imah and Topaz."

"Six hundred. Even more than last time. He grows bolder." Abba's head rested against the empty shelf. "It took five hundred for him to spare your life, so I suppose we should be grateful it isn't one thousand for Imah and Topaz. Still, I have no possible way to accumulate so much money in so little time."

"This is outrageous. We're not paying that scoundrel a single dinar. I'll speak with the centurion. Surely, he can do something to help us."

"Last time Barabbas was a wanted criminal for participating in the insurrection. This time he walks at liberty by the governor's decree. The centurion will not be able to do anything."

"There must be some way to escape him."

"He is too sly. If we move, he will follow. If we retaliate, his will outnumber us. It would only cost blood rather than dinars."

Malon slammed his fist on the table, rattling the ink jar. "Abba, we have gone through his extortion once before. I will not stand by and let him take everything from us again."

"Then you would risk the life of your imah and sister?

He is the most ruthless outlaw in the Roman Empire. He will not hesitate to kill, or even torture, them."

Malon bit his lip and inhaled a deep breath. "Even if, by some miracle, we gave him six hundred dinars, he would ask for yet more next time. At some point, we will be unable to give him what he wants. What then?"

"I don't know." Abba sighed. "For now, we must formulate a plan."

Chapter Eight

Six hundred dinars in less than a month's time? Impossible. He wasn't about to leave the fate of his mother and sister hanging on so fragile a hope. Though it would probably be futile, he had to try speaking with the centurion. Maybe the man would at least offer an idea of how to help.

After delivering the order of figs and jars to Uncle Noah, he made his way toward the garrison east of the village. He crossed the courtyard with a sidelong glance at the whipping post. The guard watched him from under eyebrows as heavy as the metal helmet on his head.

Holding his chin high, Malon didn't allow the guard's suspicion to hinder him. "I wish to speak with Centurion Dexius Vitalis, if you please."

"You?" The guard quirked one ridiculous brow.

Malon cringed. Of all times to be treated like a child. He inhaled a deep breath, puffing out his chest. The stubble beginning to emerge on his chin should help, but apparently, the guard hadn't noticed. At sixteen, he deserved more respect.

In a dramatic fashion, he looked to each of his sides, and then gave a shrug. "I don't see anyone else standing here asking to speak with the centurion. So yes, I suppose that leaves me."

The guard snorted. "I doubt the centurion has time for the likes of you."

"Tell him the man who aided in the capture of Barabbas awaits an audience, and I believe he will consider it."

"The man who — ?" The oppressive eyebrow quirked again, but this time in a more favorable fashion. "Wait here."

Malon obeyed and waited for several minutes as his conscience pricked him for his sarcastic remarks. Finally, the guard reappeared. "Follow me."

The black basalt structure engulfed him as he followed the guard down a long hallway. A few torches flickered at intervals, scarcely combating the gloom. Surely, some of the doors he passed were barracks, but what else did this mysterious building house?

"Enter." The centurion's voice filtered through the cracked door.

Malon pressed on the heavy wooden door, and its metal hinges groaned. He entered a chamber smaller than he would have expected — cold, bare, and lonely. The only redeeming quality being a small potted tree tucked away in one corner. The centurion leaned over scrolls at a large walnut table, but he looked up as Malon stepped into the light of the lamps.

"Greetings, Centurion."

"Ah, my young friend. It has been awhile since I've seen you." The centurion's pale gaze returned to the parchments, and serene features contrasted the tilt to his strong jaw. "What can I do for you?"

"You aided me once before in the capture of the criminal known as Barabbas."

"Of course. I remember."

"Barabbas has returned."

Centurion Vitalis glanced up. "Here?"

"Yes, sir. I encountered him in my shop early this morning."

"I had heard he was set at liberty during the feast. It grieved me to hear of Jesus' death. He healed a servant of mine." The parchment lowered in the centurion's hand. He peered at the wall for a moment, and his gaze seemed far away. Then he shook his head. "Barabbas has come here? What did he want?"

"Money. Does he ever want anything else?"

"Blood."

"He wants that if he cannot have the money."

"He has threatened you then?"

"My family. I have a mother and a newborn sister. He demands six hundred dinars, else he will harm them."

Vitalis winced. "Quite a sum."

"Indeed. And an impossible sum to raise before the next dark moon. Is there anything you can do for us, Centurion?"

The Roman leaned back in his chair and ran his hands through hair that reminded Malon of camel fur. "It isn't so simple this time, my young friend. Barabbas has been freed by the governor, so all the charges previously brought against him are dismissed. We have no grounds to arrest him."

"Disturbance and threatening the inhabitants of this town is not enough?"

"Unfortunately, no. He would have to perform an act of violence before we gained the authority to capture him, and by then, it would be too late."

"Can you increase the patrol in the neighborhood to prevent an issue? Maybe the presence of more soldiers would scare him off."

"I doubt it. Barabbas could walk right up to my soldiers, stick his filthy finger in their face, call them dirty names, and they could do nothing to him. He knows that. It would only challenge and embolden him."

"Is there absolutely nothing you can do?"

"I'm sorry, Malon. I would like to help you. Really, I would, but my authority only reaches so far. I would help you raise the money, but even there I'm not much help. Six hundred dinars is many times what I make in an entire year."

Malon's gaze dropped to the uneven stone floor. All his hope had rested in the centurion. When would he learn? Hang your hopes on people — like Abba, like Peter, even Jesus — and you'll hang yourself.

"So, Barabbas will come, and my father and I will die trying to protect my mother and sister."

Vitalis rose, and his armor clanked as he marched to Malon's side. He rested a hand on his shoulder. "As a centurion of Rome, I cannot help you."

Malon met his steely gaze.

"Now, as a friend…" Vitalis fell quiet, as if evaluating Malon's determination. "Come."

When the centurion turned on his heel and strode toward a door at the back of the room, Malon followed him into another small chamber. Shelves lined three of the walls, and weapons dangled in rows along the last one. A large lamp hung over a table at the center.

"This is my preparation chamber." Vitalis' voice echoed off the stone ceiling. "Here I study history, battles, methods, and tactics, and plan my approach. Perhaps we can plan yours as well."

"A plan besides die in an effort to defend my family?"

"Hopefully, yes." After selecting a scroll from the shelf, Vitalis unrolled it beneath the lamp. "First, you need an understanding of your enemy. What do you know of Barabbas?"

"He is the worst criminal in Israel. Ruthless and sly. I've heard he killed his own mother. He uses devious tactics to strike fear, never attacking outright, but unexpected, catching them off guard."

"Very true." The centurion laid the scroll out on the table. "This is a detailed documentation of the crimes Barabbas committed before we captured him. I cataloged everything so when the time came to confront him, I would know who I was challenging. How did your family become a target of his?"

"He attacked one of our caravans. His band held my father and our men off with swords while Barabbas beat me almost to death. My father finally offered him a large sum of money if he spared my life. He agreed, and he's been bleeding money from us since."

"He has visited you regularly since then?"

"Not exactly regular, but yes. He dropped by unexpectedly with another demand every few months."

"Your family is not his only victim. Barabbas led one of the bloodiest insurrections in these parts. He murdered many of his own people, besides soldiers and innocent civilians who happened to be in the wrong place at the worst time."

"What is it he wants?"

"He is a selfish and greedy man who only wants to prosper himself. He wants his every whim, and he'll do whatever it takes to get it. I think at some point in his life, Barabbas must have decided he'd never be denied anything again, and set out to make it happen."

Malon shrugged. "Seems he has succeeded. Even pardon has been granted to him."

Vitalis' gaze rested on Malon. He took half a breath, and then paused. He rested one elbow on the table. "You have in this country a small animal very much like a mouse. Are you familiar with the shrew?"

"Shrew? No, not very."

"He's a busy creature, bustling about all day with a hyper pace, but his purpose is merely to survive. To feed himself. Due to its hyperactivity, this tiny animal eats almost constantly. However, it is not an eater of grains and seeds as mice are. It preys on insects, frogs, rodents, even small snakes."

"What does this have to do with Barabbas?"

The centurion held up one finger and raised an eyebrow. "Just listen. You young lads are too impatient."

"Sorry. Go on."

"The shrew's bite contains a poison to paralyze its prey. Once paralyzed, the shrew feasts on the victim for days before it dies from the wounds."

Malon's stomach rolled. Surely, his face reflected his disgust. "How horrific."

"Truly. Now, tell me, how does this pertain to Barabbas?"

Grasping his chin, Malon thought for a moment. The shrew paralyses its prey, and then feasts on them until they bleed out and die.… Something lit like a flame in his mind. "Barabbas paralyzes with the venom of fear and drains his victims until they die."

Vitalis nodded. "Interesting too, a shrew carries a horrible stench."

"Barabbas exactly. Then how does one trap a shrew?"

"The shrew cannot be trapped as other rodents, because they are clever and not easily lured. Neither are they attracted to the same bait."

"Then how do you get rid of them?"

"The greatest predator of the shrew is the owl." The centurion's eyes narrowed. "The owl is wise and patient. They have discovered the way to capture this indomitable creature. Use the right bait, then swoop down and kill before it has a chance to react."

*****

"Are you suggesting using your mother and sister as bait?" The tips of Abba's ears glowed redder than the sunset.

"Barabbas has already set his sights on them. Besides, what other choice do we have? We cannot raise six hundred dinars."

"It's far too risky. What if we fail? Only Jehovah knows what he would do to them."

"He won't lay a finger on them. He won't live long enough."

"You really think this plan of yours will outsmart the cleverest criminal in the country? This man cheated death; he'll cheat you too. No, I think we should send Aaliyah and Topaz away until we handle Barabbas."

"What if Barabbas's spies discover our plan?" Malon

lowered his voice and glanced around to ensure no one observed him. "He would find them and slaughter them before we knew what happened."

Abba's jaw clenched. Malon was right. Abba had to know it. He paced the shop for several minutes, and then stopped before the door. "Adonai, forgive me." He faced Malon. "Very well, upon our lives, we must make this work."

*****

The leper colony had always been eerie to Malon, but it was even more when empty. He ambled through the unoccupied corridors, checking each house to ensure all the residents had vacated.

"Hello? Anyone here?" His voice echoed off the empty hut's stone walls. Good. Even this last section was as empty as his rumbling stomach.

"Malon?"

"Here, Abba." He turned as his father trotted down the lane.

"Everything is set. The oil has been spread, and we've placed barrels of it in strategic locations. The lepers who are too sick to help are settling into the caves."

Malon faced the cliffs beyond the leper village. "Were

any of the lepers well enough to contribute? How many men do we have in all?"

"Three or four. Counting them, Vitalis' servants, and the men from town—twenty. Aside from me and you."

"Where is Imah? I need to explain the arrangement one last time so she is clear."

"She was helping those settling in the caves, but she should be along shortly." Abba shifted, and a pained expression twisted his face. "I can't go through with this, son."

Malon frowned. It was too late to turn back now. "We have to, Abba. I promise I won't let any harm befall them."

"This is Barabbas, son! You can't make such a promise."

"I'll be defending them with my sword. We picked the perfect location. It is too narrow for them to get through and harm Imah or the babe before they could escape."

Abba shook his head. His teeth grated together.

Malon drew in a steadying breath. "We have no other options. We can run, but Barabbas would find us. This way, we actually get rid of him. We'll be saving not only ourselves, but the entire nation."

"What if you don't get out in time?"

As if he hadn't wondered the same question a hundred times. He looked away. He still didn't have a good answer. "I will."

A rat scurried from one of the huts and disappeared behind an oil barrel. If only he felt as confident as his reply. The rumbling in his stomach ceased, replaced by nausea.

"Tyrus? Malon?"

"Here, Imah." Malon stepped into the main alley as Imah approached, cradling Topaz.

"There you are. The lepers are settled. I've brought some bread and cheese if you're hungry. The sun will set soon."

"I know. We haven't much more time." At least he could move forward and end the discussion with Abba. He directed his words to Imah. "There will be no moon tonight, so we can expect Barabbas. I don't know how long it will take him to figure out that we're here, but we need to be prepared before dusk. Do you know what you are to do?"

"Yes, my son, you've told me several times."

"Right. Can you run carrying Topaz?"

"Tyrus was kind enough to fashion a cradle of sorts, so I can carry her on my back. We'll be fine." Imah gave Abba one of those meaningful gazes Malon wouldn't understand until he had a woman of his own.

"All right. Grab some bread, and let's get into

position." Abba waved them on.

Imah handed out the bread, and they blessed it and ate in silence. The prodding feeling that this may be their last meal together squelched any conversation.

Malon brushed his hands on his tunic. "Let's get ready. I don't want to look flustered when he appears."

Abba gently gathered Topaz from Imah and peered at her perfect baby features. "I love you, my daughter. Abba will see you soon. Be good for Imah."

"Goo."

He planted a kiss on her pudgy cheek and wiped a tear from his own. He returned Topaz and pulled Imah into his embrace. He held her tightly before drawing back enough to kiss her. "If anything goes wrong, cry out, and I'll come as quickly as I can."

Malon averted his head as Abba bent toward her again.

"Son, take care of these two and yourself. I demand that you all get out of this place alive. You understand?"

"Yes, sir."

"I still think I should be the one staying here in the midst of Barabbas and the flames."

"I am the one who last interacted with him. Besides, you need to oversee the archers and make sure Imah gets to safety. It's the best role for you."

A deep breath, and Abba nodded. He placed a hand on Malon's shoulder and bowed his head. "Adonai, please protect my family. Help our plan meet success, and bring us through safely. Amen."

"Amen."

Abba's moist dark eyes locked with Malon's. "I love you, my son. God be with you."

"I love you too."

Abba turned and, with stiff shoulders and reluctant steps, walked away.

*****

Malon's palm sweated against his sword handle. He removed it long enough to wipe his hand on his tunic, and then rested it there again. He wouldn't be caught off guard when the shrew appeared.

They'd been in position waiting for what seemed an eternity. Had it ever been so dark? He hated nights with no moon. It had become difficult to see. His eyes played tricks on him, casting dancing shadows in empty places. He couldn't let Barabbas sneak up on him again. This time, with Imah and Topaz behind him, he had too much to lose.

Had something gone wrong? Had Barabbas learned of

their plan? Would he somehow sneak into the colony another way? Would the vermin's fear of contamination keep him from coming at all?

Clink.

Something before him moved. Shivers prickled his skin, creeping up the back of his neck. "Who's there?"

Imah caught his cue, and a torch sizzled to life, shedding light all around them. Barabbas stood like an angry rodent. Torchlight gleamed off the dagger in his hand.

Malon inhaled. His plan better work.

Chapter Nine

"You didn't think I'd dare follow you here, eh, scum? Thought I'd be afraid of the lepers?"

Malon drew his sword from his sheath, the vibrations fueling his nerves. "You impress me, Barabbas. You've proved yourself a coward in every other instance."

The insult produced the desired effect, and Barabbas's face turned crimson. "I think it's safe to assume you don't have the money. So I get to torture your family before your eyes, and then rid the earth of your miserable existence. Or maybe, I'll just cut off your feet and gouge out your eyes so you can rot your life away like I did in Pilate's prison."

"I've bested you once. What makes you think I can't do it again?"

Barabbas snapped his fingers. Filthy men emerged

from every nearby building. They flanked him with arms folded across their chests. "Don't be a fool. I came prepared to take the vengeance I've been dreaming of for three years."

Malon glanced behind him, hoping Imah had backed up and escaped. He had to keep Barabbas's attention fixed on him so she could. "Not man enough to take on a lad of sixteen by yourself, I see. You need a full cohort of ruffians."

"On the contrary. I intend to use you as a training exercise. After I finish with your mother and sister, that is." Barabbas pointed his chin beyond Malon.

No. Imah was still there. She was supposed to have retreated already. He had to find a way for her to back out safely. "I see. Well, I hate to embarrass you in front of all your men. Back up, Imah. We may need some room for this."

His mother's footsteps shuffled then grew fainter, and he shot up a prayer that she could make it out before Barabbas tore him limb for limb. As soon as she exited the colony, Abba and the others would release flaming arrows to ignite the oil. Until then, he only needed to refrain from being killed.

The villain's eyes focused in on his, and he drew his sword, the rough metal grating against the sheath. A well-worn blade. How many lives had it taken? Spreading his feet apart, Malon prepared for his opponent's advance.

Barabbas's smile exposed rotting teeth as he mimicked Malon's movements. "We'll have some fun with the boy. What do you say, men?"

Low chuckles emanated from their onlookers.

Please, Adonai, I need a little help.

Faking confidence, Malon slapped at Barabbas's blade with his own. "Watch your grip, old man. You may lose your hold on life along with your pathetic excuse for a weapon."

Black eyes smoldering, Barabbas lunged. Knowing his strength was no match, Malon dodged the blow, and the thief hurtled into the side of a hut.

Malon smirked as a grunt was forced from Barabbas. "Speed and strength are no match for agility and wit."

With an angry cry, Barabbas attacked again. This time his blade connected with Malon's, sending a spark to the sand at their feet. Barabbas's furious strength was more than he could match. His sword faltered, gliding toward the ground. He took several steps back, preparing for another blow.

A high whistle pierced the air, and flaming arrows rained down around them. They hit their mark, and soon a ring of fire surrounded them. HaShem be praised, Imah and Topaz had made it out safely. Another whistling volley sent arrows plunking into barrels of oil, which exploded, spreading the flames quicker than before. Time to make his retreat.

He lunged at Barabbas, delivering several hard blows. Their swords locked in close proximity, and his opponent's foul breath puffed against his face. Barabbas narrowed his eyes and swept his elbow down. The delivered blow reeled Malon toward the flames.

His tunic sleeve caught fire. He dropped to the ground and rolled, smothering the flame and distancing himself. He picked himself up and swiped at his bleeding nose. The flames spread rapidly. If he was to escape, he'd have to soon.

Barabbas darted toward him again, but Malon jumped first and delivered a blow with his sword hilt to the thief's chest. He didn't wait to see Barabbas stumble backward. He ran. Only one place to elude the fire…and he had to get there now. The cries of Barabbas's men escalated, their panic rising with their voices.

Air caught in Malon's lungs as he tried to run. They'd left a gap near the longest hut. He skidded to a stop. There was no gap.

Panic nipped at his heels. His plan was failing. Would this be his end? Sweat trickled down the back of his neck.

Flames leapt from one hut roof to another, crackling and popping as they went and leaving no bare areas on the ground. In about two minutes, the rest of the oil would catch fire, and then everything — and everyone — inside the circle would be consumed.

His lungs burned, and coughing seized him. How was he going to get out?

Wham! He hit the ground, and his breath rushed from him. Barabbas's gigantic form crushed him into the sand, grinding kernels against his raw skin, and Malon struggled for air. *Do something! Now.* Fast before he passed out. He curled both of his legs up and, with all the strength he could muster, slammed his feet against Barabbas's chest.

Lord God, help me.

Groaning from the effort, he flung Barabbas off and sprang to his feet. The outlaw snarled like an enraged beast and rolled over. With no other choice, Malon sprinted away. His mind raced as quickly as his feet. What could he do? The flames were closing in fast.

He raced toward them. He'd have to try to run through them. He closed his eyes and leapt into the flames.

Chapter Ten

He hit the ground hard. His tunic clung to the melted skin on his legs and arms, but he rolled anyway, desperate to douse the flames. A pain, so great he would cry, seized him, but he hadn't the breath to do so. Ignoring the smoldering in his hands and knees, he scrambled farther from the flames and laid against the cool earth as tears trickled from his eyes. He was safe. And Barabbas was not.

He raised his head to look at the blaze consuming the leper colony. The cries had ceased. Barabbas and his men had perished.

Relief washed over him and alleviated his suffering. *Thank You, Lord.*

"Malon?" His father's panicked voice reached him.

"Here, Abba." He winced as he sat up.

"I feared you hadn't made it out." Abba scuttled to his

side and dropped to his knees. He placed his hands on each side of Malon's face. "You're badly burned."

"I'm better off than Barabbas."

His words didn't ease the concern in Abba's dark eyes. "Can you walk?"

"I think so…if you'll give me a few moments to catch my breath."

Abba plopped to the ground beside him and gazed at the smoke ascending from the colony. "You have no conception of how hard it was for me to know you were in the midst of the inferno."

"Where is Imah?"

"Waiting on the hill with the others. When we saw you come out through the fire, I asked her to stay behind. I couldn't risk her getting close to the blaze."

Malon let out a breath. He'd assumed she reached safety, but hearing Abba confirm it released the tension from his shoulders.

"I once lost a sister to fire."

Shock washed over Malon as he stared at his father. His expression had turned gloomy.

"You did?"

Abba nodded. "When my family fled Rome, the soldiers set fire to the hut we were lodging in. Topaz never came out."

"Topaz? Then you named my sister after yours?"

"Yes. It seemed fitting. I thought I conquered all those old fears, but when your mother, Topaz, and you were in the midst of a fiery plan, it was all I could do to stay calm. I haven't felt panic like that since the night my sister died." He blinked the moisture from his eyes. "I praise Adonai you're all safe."

As much as he hated to end this tender moment, the pain of his burns grew worse by the second. "I think I'm ready to go now."

Abba stood and helped Malon to his feet. "Easy now."

"I'm all right. My legs and arms are scorched, so as long as you don't touch me, I think I can make it home."

They turned toward the city walked a few paces.

"I will kill you, Malon Ben-Tyrus!" A bloodcurdling cry warbled from the smoldering ashes. "If it's the last thing I do, I'll kill you and your family for this."

The hair on the back of his neck prickled. The voice seemed to echo all around them. One thing was certain: it was Barabbas.

*****

How did Barabbas survive the fire? In his waking, the thought haunted Malon. And in his dreams, Barabbas stood over his family with his hideous grin and a jagged dagger, ready to strike. Each time, Malon awakened with sweat puddled on his heaving chest.

Why was it that no matter how hard he tried, everything turned out poorly? Why did terrible things always happen to him? And why was he powerless to stop it?

His seared skin was healing — thanks to Savta's salve — but the burn in his heart bothered him most. His entire life he'd imagined that one day he would join the Messiah and fight to rid his people of Rome's oppression and set things straight in Jerusalem, casting out all those corrupt scribes and Pharisees. But now, Jesus was dead.

"You hear my Father's call, Malon. He will use you and your youth for His glory. One day you will go where I lead you, but this is not that day."

He recalled Jesus' words so clearly. As if they'd been said yesterday. He had been so sure they would come true. What did it matter now? Jesus failed him, as had Peter, and worse, he failed himself. He hardly knew who he was anymore. What was the point of living, if your life had no purpose?

Keep Barabbas from harming your family. That was his purpose for now.

He shoved a crate into the wagon bed and, with it,

thrust away those thoughts. He would have plenty of time to think later as he lay awake in the darkness. For now, he needed to sell these goods in Bethany. He'd been restricted to bed rest for the past few weeks, even though they needed the funds from his sales to purchase materials to repair the leper colony. Once they made the repairs and improvements, it would benefit the lepers enough to make up for the inconvenience of vacating for a few weeks.

"Good afternoon, Malon."

He jumped at the voice behind him and whirled around to Rabbi Ben-Elior standing with a tentative smile on his lips. "Rabbi, I'm surprised to see you."

"Yes, it has been some time."

The man had gall to show his face at the shop. He certainly wasn't here to purchase anything. He made it clear he would not support their business when they refused to denounce Jesus and he ruined Topaz's dedicational feast. Maybe since Jesus was dead, he decided to be sensible. "Is there something I can help you with?"

"Is your father inside?"

"Yes. Would you like me to call him for you?"

"No. I will step into the shop to speak with him. That is a large load here. Where are you taking it?"

"Bethany."

The rabbi poked his nose over the edge of the cart. "You ought to make a nice profit off the sales of such goods."

"I pray Adonai will bless it. We'll be using the profits to repair the leper colony."

"The leper colony?"

"Yes, sir. It was damaged by a fire." Not sure how many details he should disclose, Malon left it at that.

Ben-Elior straightened his robes. "I know your family has sympathy for lepers, given your mother's situation, but aren't you aware leprosy is HaShem's judgment on these people? To help them is to intervene with Adonai's correction."

Malon stared at him. Could this man really believe what he just said? Did he truly think it a sin to aid the lepers? How was he to respond to such a remark?

"Never mind." The rabbi gave a wave of his hand. "I will speak to your father regarding this matter."

After Ben-Elior disappeared into the shop, Malon gathered the water and food Imah prepared for his journey. He grasped his sword and strapped it to his side. He'd be traveling the roads alone, and with Barabbas roaming…His stomach churned.

He patted the donkey's neck. "Ready, boy?"

The animal bobbed its head.

Malon winced as he grasped the reins in his left hand and climbed into the wagon. He wiggled on the wooden bench. Bouncing against the wooden bench with healing burns would turn to agony quickly. He grabbed one of the blankets from the crates and folded it to provide a little cushion.

As Malon raised his hand to flick the reins, Rabbi Ben-Elior exited the shop wearing a frown. He paused at the doorway. "Consider what I've said, Tyrus. Adonai cannot bless your business if you rob from Him." With that, he turned on his heel and walked away.

Abba emerged from the shop. His nostrils flared as he inhaled deeply and gripped the cart's side.

"I suppose the conversation didn't go well."

"Such impudence," Abba murmured. "I don't know how I was such good friends with the man for so long."

"What is it he wanted?"

"He was paying us a courteous visit. He'd noticed that our giving at the temple has decreased, and he wanted to make sure we were doing well. I told him our profits had been low, and we had increased expenses. He proceeded to tell me God was not blessing our business because we are giving aid to the lepers."

Malon's jaw dropped. "He didn't say that, did he?"

Abba let out a long breath. "He did."

"Unbelievable. There is no end to the Pharisees' meddling."

"He says we should take the profits from your trip to Bethany and donate them to the synagogue. Then the priests would accept us back into the congregation, and God would restore his blessing to our home and business. I suppose since Jesus is dead, he thinks the battle is over and was hoping to make amends."

Gritting his teeth, Malon chose not to respond. He didn't wish to say evil about the rabbi, but the entire lot of scribes and Pharisees had grown corrupt with greed and pride. "Tell me, Abba, what is the difference between the Romans and their oppressive taxes and the Pharisees with their alms soliciting?"

After a long moment, Abba replied, "I wish I could answer you, my son, but I know not what to say."

Malon gripped the reins, mirroring the constricting in his chest. "What is the difference between Barabbas's threats and Rabbi Ben-Eilor's 'request'?"

Abba winced. "Ben-Elior has not threatened our family."

"No? He says we will be condemned to eternal punishment and earthly trouble if we don't give them the money. Isn't this the same as Barabbas? Or maybe even worse?"

With a hard swallow, Abba shook his head. "I don't know. For now, you need to get going."

Biting his lip, Malon snapped the reins and clicked his tongue. The cart lurched into motion. "Shalom, Abba."

"Safe travels, my son."

Chapter Eleven

Malon breathed a prayer of thanksgiving. He'd managed to sell all the goods and made plenty of profits to repair the leper's huts. As soon as he finished loading the empty crates into the wagon, he could return home for a good meal and some rest.

"Well, if it isn't my young Jewish pack mule."

Closing his eyes, he pleaded for patience as he recognized the antagonizing voice. "Good afternoon, Centurion."

He turned and faced Gallus, who wore his familiar smirk. The centurion's pride was so strong, Malon could smell it. Or maybe it was just the donkey manure the centurion was standing in.

"What brings a boy like you so far from home? I would think you wouldn't want to spend a night away from your mother."

The metallic sensation of blood flooded his mouth as he bit his tongue.

Gallus removed his helmet and wiped sweat from his forehead. "I'm thirsty. Fetch me water from the well."

"You don't know where the well is in this town?"

"If I do or don't, what difference does it make?" The centurion's eyes, a brownish green like the mess he'd stepped in, gleamed.

Even my donkey can get water for himself, but I suppose you possess less intelligence than he, so I'll oblige. Malon swallowed the retort. It would only get him whipped again — something he didn't need, especially with his burns still healing. He picked up a water bucket from his cart and headed toward the well. How outrageous the Roman servitude laws were. If the soldiers were present to protect them, it would be another thing, but they were there for the sole purpose of enforcing their own despicable laws. Nothing more.

When he returned, Gallus was sitting on the driver's bench of the wagon. Irritation puckered Malon's lips, but he forced them into a line. At least his cart was empty, leaving nothing for the rouge to steal. "Your water, Centurion."

"Is it cold?"

"As cold as it can be. We've no running streams to draw from."

Gallus slouched lower on the seat and held out his hand, as if expecting Malon to act as butler and hand him a cup.

Malon dropped the bucket, water sloshing onto the dirt at his feet. "I've done my duty and brought the water. You have no right to deter me. Please extract yourself from my property, and I'll be on my way."

"I would have thought you learned your lesson about being so pert toward an officer of the Imperial Army. Need I revisit that lesson?"

"I said please. You ought to be happy. It's more than you deserve. You can whip me for nothing. I've violated no law." His nails gouged into his palms, but he managed to keep his voice calm.

The centurion sat up and jumped from the cart. "Have you paid the duties on the goods you've sold here?"

"We pay the taxes at the duty house in Capernaum."

"Ah, but you've conducted your business here in Bethany. Therefore you must pay a tax to the city for soliciting our business."

"That is preposterous. I've never heard of such a thing."

"No? Well, you may have been violating the city duty

laws then. For a cart this size, the duties are fifteen dinars."

"Where is the collector? I will speak with him and remit payment to him alone."

"I will collect the tax." Gallus lifted his chin. "Unless you want me to arrest you for not paying tribute."

"Soldiers don't collect the taxes. I will pay the collector only."

Gallus stepped closer, a sour expression on his pale Roman features. "As the centurion in command here in Bethany, I enforce the tax. Pay me, or face the consequences."

Malon held the centurion's gaze for several long moments. His stomach twisted into a knot. He did not want to give Gallus a single mite, but what else could he do? If he really was the centurion in command, he could haul Malon to prison, and no one would stop him. By no possibility was the charge a legitimate tax. The money wouldn't go to the treasury, but to Gallus' tab at the inn.

Gritting his teeth, Malon reached into his pouch, withdrew fifteen dinars, and dropped them into the centurion's waiting palm.

Gallus counted the coins with a finger, and then grinned. "All right then, you're free to go."

Face hot, Malon climbed into the cart and drove out of the city. Even with the open space all around him, he felt claustrophobic. He couldn't do anything without Barabbas, the priests, or a Roman soldier getting in his way. Each one wanted a portion of his money pouch, leaving little for his family. This was the tyranny the Messiah was promised to liberate his people from. But Jesus was dead. Should he look for another to come? Right now the promise of the Messiah seemed so distant, it was nonexistent.

If only Simon Peter and the other disciples had withstood the band that came to carry Jesus away. If only they'd fought for him. If only he'd gone to Jerusalem along with Jesus. Contemplating these scenarios didn't help. Rather Malon only grew more irritable.

When he arrived at the shop, he took the money pouch and plopped it on the desk in front of Abba.

His father picked up the bag and jingled the coins. "How much?"

"Fifteen dinars less than it should be."

Abba's dark brows lowered into a scowl. "What do you mean?"

"The centurion walked up as I was leaving Bethany. He told me there was a duty to sell inside the city. He forced me to pay him fifteen dinars."

"There was no tax collector?"

"No, sir. Only the centurion."

Abba growled. "Insanity. Can't we do anything without someone taking our money?"

"Will we still have enough to repair the leper colony? Those people can't stay in the caves forever."

Abba frowned at the logs. He was silent for a moment, pointing to different figures, and then scratched out a tally at the bottom. "There's enough. We won't be able to do all the improvements we hoped, but we can make it inhabitable again. I'll see about the supplies tomorrow. You let the men know we'll begin work after the Sabbath."

Someone behind them rapped on the door. The door was open, and Peter stood in the doorway. "Am I interrupting?"

What was he doing here? "Only slightly," Malon muttered. His annoyance at the sight of Peter bothered him. He shouldn't carry a grudge. Then again, why not? The disciple allowed Jesus to be crucified and cowered in a corner during the aftermath. He wouldn't as much as leave the room to return to Capernaum. That had been almost two months ago, but it still roused something inside him. Malon turned his back and moved toward the shelves. Peter wasn't here to see him anyway. He'd want to speak with Abba.

Peter stepped inside, followed by a young woman. Petronilla. Heat flushed Malon's face as he recalled his last...encounter with Peter's daughter.

"Good evening, Simon." Abba shot Malon a warning glance. *Be polite.* "I wasn't aware you'd returned from Jerusalem."

"I arrived yesterday. I've come for my family. We are relocating to Jerusalem."

Malon couldn't help looking at Peter, and the disciple caught his gaze. "I've come to invite Malon to join us."

Simon's entire family had lived in Capernaum for generations. Now he was leaving? And asking Malon along?

"Why?" He hadn't meant to sound so trite, but there it was.

"When you came to me in Jerusalem," Peter rushed on, seemingly undeterred by his tone. "you said you wanted to be a disciple of Jesus. Said you felt a call to follow him."

"What does it matter? Jesus is dead."

A smile parted the fisherman's scruffy beard. "There you're wrong. Jesus is alive."

Malon took a step back and narrowed his eyes. "You're the one who assured me of his death."

"It is true that he died, but he is dead no longer. He is risen, as he said he would."

Something was different about Peter's eyes. A light gleamed from them, even in the shop's darkness. Come to think of it, his entire face looked different. What was it?

"I've seen him, Malon. Jesus is alive."

What a claim. Peter believed it, for certain. His belief twinkled in his brown eyes. Malon tore his gaze away from Peter's, only to meet Petronilla's, which didn't help his flustered stomach.

"I don't know what you think you saw, but men don't come back to life after being crucified by the Romans. I won't allow you to make a fool of me again."

Petronilla arched one of her sculptured brows. No doubt thinking he did well enough at making a fool of himself, he didn't need her father's assistance.

"True, men don't," Peter insisted. "The Messiah…he has. Andrew has also seen him, and the rest of the disciples. He has appeared to us many times."

"Appeared? Forgive me, but you sound as if you've gone mad."

Another warning look from Abba.

Malon huffed in a breath and turned toward the shelves.

"Simon, why don't you sit and explain. From the beginning." Abba motioned to the chair opposite his desk. "Malon, won't you get a seat for Simon's daughter?"

Usually, Malon would have reminded his father that the fisherman liked to be called Peter, but right then, he didn't care. He stepped outside, inhaled the fresh air, and grabbed the stool from beneath the canopy. Setting it on the wooden shop floor, he slid it toward Petronilla with his foot.

"Thank you," she whispered, her voice as soft and sweet as honey.

He lifted his chin in answer and plopped down on a barrel, welcoming the distracting pain from the burns on his legs. She eased onto the stool, as if concerned he'd given her one with a loose leg. Folding his arms across his chest, he focused on Peter.

The disciple met his eyes with a confident gaze. "Malon, do you remember the prophecy in the Psalm that says, 'Thou will not leave my soul in hell, neither will thou suffer thy Holy One to see corruption?'"

"I remember."

"Do you know how long it takes a body to begin to decay?"

He shook his head.

"Three days. How long was the prophet Jonah in the belly of the whale?"

"Three days."

Peter's head bobbed. "Shortly before his death, Jesus spoke to us and said 'even as Jonah was in the belly of the whale for three days and nights, so shall the Son of Man be three days and nights in the heart of the earth.' Later he said again 'we will go to Jerusalem, and the Son of Man will be delivered into the hands of sinful men, and be crucified, and on the third day rise again.' I didn't understand when he said these things, but after I saw him, all things became clear."

Abba rubbed his chin. "You're saying Jesus was dead for three days, as prophesied?"

"Yes. Listen, after Malon left us in Jerusalem, the women went to the tomb to anoint the body with spices. When they got to the tomb, the stone was rolled away, and Jesus' body was gone. They feared someone had stolen the body, but an angel appeared and told them Jesus had risen from the dead as he promised."

Malon held up a hand. "If the women were half as grief stricken at the tomb as they were the day I came to you in Jerusalem, nothing they say can be relied upon. They were beside themselves."

"Perhaps you could discount their story if they were the only ones, but there is more." Peter's countenance lit unlike Malon had ever seen in him. "The women came running to us and told what had happened. So John and I ran to the tomb, and we found everything as the women had said, except we didn't see the angel. When I entered the tomb, I looked at the place where I laid the body only days before, and the napkin was folded." Peter paused, as if this was supposed to be significant.

Abba frowned and leaned back. "I don't understand. Why is that important?"

Taking a steadying breath, Peter continued, "I served the Master many times. When a disciple is serving his Master, and the Master arises from the table, he will leave his napkin behind. If the napkin is thrown onto the table without care, he is finished. If the napkin is folded, he is coming back."

Malon blinked.

"Don't you see? The angel told the women to come and tell me what they'd seen. When I went to the tomb, the napkin that had covered Jesus face was folded. He was saying to me, 'I am coming back.' Then I believed he had indeed arisen from the dead, as he said he would."

"I'm sorry, Simon." Abba rested his hands on the desk. "But it is going to take more than a napkin for me to believe a man has come back to life."

"Is it really so hard to believe?" Peter ran a hand through his tangled, sandy hair. "Did he not raise Lazarus? Did he not raise the widow's son at Nain? How then is it difficult to believe he raised himself?"

"Never before has a man raised himself to life."

"We speak of the Messiah, Tyrus. Never before has a

man had the power of God. Some days after the women saw him, Jesus appeared to us in the house where we stayed. All the doors were locked, and suddenly, he was amongst us. He sat and talked with us. Ate with us. Touched us. Showed us the scars in his hands and side. He even prepared fish for us on the banks of the Galilee. I tell you Jesus is alive."

Malon's gaze shifted from Peter's ardent face to Petronilla's. She watched her father with an eager expression. Apparently, she believed his tale. Something about her made Malon's heart knock on his chest, as if reminding him it was still there. He dropped his gaze, picked up a string from the floor, and twirled it between his fingertips.

"If Jesus is alive, where is he now?" he asked without looking up.

"Forty days after his resurrection, we walked with Jesus to a mountain, and before our eyes, he was lifted up into the sky. He told us to wait in Jerusalem until we received power from on high. Then he was gone into heaven."

"I believe in miracles, Peter, but you must understand this is difficult to conceive."

"Malon, when you came to Jerusalem, you believed Jesus to be the Messiah. What made you change your mind?"

"Last time you invited me to Jerusalem, it was because you believed the Messiah — God with us — to be living among us. What point is there now?"

"You're right. Emmanuel is no longer living among us, but *in* us."

"They killed him. The Messiah was to restore all things, to bring liberty. He didn't."

"Not in the way you thought he should, but he did fulfill his mission. I didn't understand while he was still alive, but during the time after his resurrection, he explained everything. Jesus' kingdom is not of this world, but in heaven. He came and suffered the punishment for our sins, just as was prophesied by the prophet Isaiah. That's why he had to die. Then he rose again to prove he is the Christ."

"He told you to wait in Jerusalem?" Abba bent forward.

"Yes, so we waited in the upper room where Malon met us. One day, there came a strange noise into the room. Like a mighty wind, but all outside was still. Then a tongue of fire entered the room, and it rested over each of us. I cannot tell you what happened, but everything changed. Never have I experienced anything like it. Some of us began speaking in other tongues. We ran into the street, because we were no longer afraid. We had to share the news of Christ and his resurrection with everyone in Jerusalem, so we ran toward the temple and began preaching."

"You?" Malon's question emerged as a snort. "Ran out into the street and began preaching? Last time I saw you, you were too terrified to show your face in the city."

"It is the power of the Holy Ghost, Malon. It changed me."

"Truly, it has." Petronilla leaned over and rested her head on Peter's shoulder, a hint of a smile touching her lips. "My father is so changed, we hardly know him anymore."

Malon didn't know how to reply.

Abba rose and rounded the table. "So, what you are telling us is the power of God has come down and is now tabernacling inside men?"

"Yes, it is as Jesus said, 'Lo, I am with you always, even in you until the end of the age.' This is the fulfillment of the prophecy given by Joel, 'Behold I will pour out my spirit upon all flesh, and your sons and daughters shall prophesy, and your old men shall dream dreams.'"

Malon recalled similar Scripture passages in the Psalms and the book of Isaiah. He had always wondered what they meant. Perhaps he would soon know.

"If the Messiah is truly alive and his spirit is dwelling in you, then you will do the same works he did." Abba crossed his arms.

"The same thought crossed my mind, and I wondered if it was true. John and I went to the temple, and sitting at the Beautiful Gate was a man who had been lame since birth. He asked alms of us, but we had none. Such compassion for the man filled me, I could have cried for him. Then I felt compelled to speak to him. 'Silver and gold I don't have,' I said. 'But what I do have, I will give to you. In the name of Jesus Christ of Nazareth, arise and walk.' Then the man's legs straightened before our eyes, and he stood up and went leaping about the temple."

Abba's eyes widened. "A man lame from birth?"

"Indeed. If you do not believe me, come to our house, and Andrew will testify as well." Peter pinned Malon with his gaze. "Come to Jerusalem, and you can hear the testimony of the other disciples. More than one hundred of us can attest to the truth of my words."

Malon searched Peter's eyes, not seeing the same grieving man he'd left in Jerusalem. Still, should he trust him? He had relied on Peter, and he'd failed him.

"I have a leper colony to rebuild and a family to consider. Barabbas was released upon Jesus' death, and he has threatened my mother and sister."

Disappointment and concern etched lines in Peter's face. "Very well, but I ask you to think about what I've said. We leave for Jerusalem in three days' time, on the first day of the week. If you reconsider, you are welcome to come with me. In the meantime, we will pray for you and your family." Peter rose and held out his hand to his daughter. "Come along, Pet. Your mother will be waiting."

Petronilla glanced at Malon from beneath her long lashes as she rose. She bowed her head toward Abba. "Shalom," she said in her small voice, and then followed her father from the shop.

Malon watched them go, irritation pinching his gut. He waited a few moments. Then he could no longer bite back his frustration. "Can you believe he would ask me to Jerusalem again? After what happened last time?"

Abba leaned against the desk, silent.

"He shooed me away with no answers. No direction. He cowered behind excuses and allowed Jesus to be killed and his followers to scatter."

"Tell me, my son, does it bother you more that Peter came to ask you to join him, or that there really is something different about him?"

The question hung in the air. Air suddenly hot, thick, and suffocating in the cloistered shop. "I ..." Sweat beaded on Malon's nose. He walked to the window and opened the shutters, his shoulders loosening when a slight breeze tickled his face. "He is an undependable coward. I wouldn't go with him if it promised enough money to buy Capernaum."

One of Abba's dark brows rose. "Simon discovered he was wrong. He came to make it right. What else would you expect a good man to do?"

When Malon had no answer, Abba stepped closer. "Don't speak ill of him. Simon is my friend, and I believe him to be a good man. Speak evil of him, and you do of me as well."

Managing a nod, Malon replied, "Yes, Abba, I apologize." Yet it didn't help the perplexity and frustration boiling over as bile in his throat. Something was different about Simon Peter. He didn't know what it was, and that bothered him more than he wished to admit.

Chapter Twelve

"You're so quiet tonight, Malon."

He shifted as Imah's soft brown eyes watched him from across the table.

"You are usually more interactive during recitation and family prayer. Are you feeling well?"

"I'm fine, Imah. Only weary, is all." He managed a small smile he hoped would reassure her.

"Is there something on your mind tonight?" Abba asked. His tallit draped his shoulders, and lamplight flickered against the open prayer scroll in his hands.

Malon blinked. How sheepish he felt. He couldn't even say what they had been speaking of for the past quarter of an hour. "No, nothing specific. I'm sorry. I'll curb my distraction. What are we reciting tonight?"

"From the prophecy of Joel. This is a passage I was

taught when I was about your age." Abba continued, "'And ye shall know that I am in the midst of Israel, and that I am Jehovah your God, and there is none else; and my people shall never be put to shame. And it shall come to pass afterward, that I will pour out my Spirit upon all flesh; and your sons and your daughters shall prophesy, your old men shall dream dreams, your young men shall see visions: and also upon the servants and upon the handmaids in those days will I pour out my Spirit. And I will show wonders in the heavens and in the earth: blood, and fire, and pillars of smoke.'"

A frown darkened Malon's vision. Why did Abba have to pick that Scripture? "Do you then agree with Peter's explanation of this portion, Abba?"

Abba looked at him and cocked his head. "Perhaps. I thought this a good recitation for this evening since it was fresh in our minds. I wanted to go back to the Scriptures he referenced and discuss them as a family. I do believe Jesus must be the Messiah, even though things did not end as we — or I — thought they should. It could be I missed something, or perhaps the events were not to unfold as I, or even the priests, thought they would. One thing I know for certain, the prophets told us to look for the sign of the Messiah, and Jesus demonstrated it. It is as he said in his own words, 'If you do not believe me, believe the works.' I have both seen and believe the works that Jesus of Nazareth did."

"Pardon me, Abba, but that seems a bold statement for you to make. Especially considering how reluctant you are to proclaim it in public."

A shadow passed over Abba's features. "I have a family to provide for. If flaunting my beliefs will harm my business, then I will keep them to myself, even as Esther and Mordecai did."

"Then you believe Jesus has risen from the dead, as Peter says?"

"I cannot say for certain, but if the signs and marvels that Jesus did are now being repeated by the disciples, it must mean he is indeed alive."

"All I've seen out of the disciples is nothing but…" Malon bit his lip, refusing to repeat the offense of speaking against Peter. He took a deep breath and scraped at the dirt beneath his fingernails. "I've not seen them act as Jesus did."

"Well, you're going to get the chance. I'm sending you to Jerusalem."

His head shot up. "Why? Would you force me to accept Peter's invitation?"

"No, there is a shipment coming on your uncle's ship. I was going to send Kish to retrieve the load at Caesarea and take it to Jerusalem, but he'll need help. So I've decided to send you."

Malon winced. It seemed a cruel punishment. "As much as I will enjoy seeing Uncle Tavor, don't you think Kish can take the goods to Jerusalem himself?"

"No. The caravan will be too large, and Caleb is busy keeping up with the Herodium shipments. Besides, I can see your heart will not be settled until you go to Jerusalem for yourself and witness what is happening with Jesus' followers. I too want to hear the report, and I'm trusting you to bring me a true account."

With a resigned sigh, Malon held up his hands. "As you wish, Abba. When do I leave?"

"Tomorrow."

*****

The stench of camels and the grit clinging to every inch of Malon's body was one of the main reasons he detested long trips. Especially in the midst of the summer months, traveling the deserted distance between Caesarea and Jerusalem was torture. To his great relief, he hadn't run into Barabbas or any other thieves. What had become of Barabbas? How had he survived the fire? More importantly, how long would it keep him away, and what would he dare do when he returned? If the cloud these questions created provided shade, Malon might have been glad for them.

Wiping the sweat from his forehead, he tugged the camel's reins and guided it toward the Cardo marketplace. Behind him, seven camels ambled along, with Kish bringing up the rear. Praise be to Adonai they'd had no difficulty on this trip.

Chattering voices, and the stench of penned animals, reached Malon before they rounded the corner into the marketplace. Beggars sat in central locations, their tattered, filthy clothes marring the walkway. Harlots haunted the street corners with their tinkling gold bracelets and slit tunics. So many people milled about. One could get lost amidst the throng or trampled underfoot. Jerusalem's swarm, though usual, left him uneasy. He didn't like crowds. He could never tell who was watching, and it was easy for someone to take him off guard.

He and Kish worked all day, unloading the camels and preparing for morning commerce. After checking the camels into the stables, he wandered to the well. Many women came to draw water for the night, but he hesitated to ask just anyone about the disciples.

An older woman with a kind face smiled at him, and

he decided she was as good as any. "Excuse me, do you know where I can find the followers of Jesus?"

Her face puckered, as if he'd insulted her. "I wouldn't know. I'm not one of them. Stay away if you have any sense. They've all gone mad." She lifted her water pot and turned up her nose as she walked away.

Well then. If they all behave like that, I'll never find Peter.

He waited for half an hour longer and was about to give up when a familiar figure slipped from an alley and came toward the well. Malon wondered how her slim form didn't buckle beneath the weight of the clay pot on her head.

She steadied the pot with both of her slender hands. Her copper eyes caught his and widened. "Malon?"

"Shalom, Petronilla. I…" He bit his tongue. He was going to say he'd been hoping he would see her — well, not her exactly, but someone he knew — anyway, that would sound…awkward. He groped for another way to say what he meant. "I've been looking, uh, for your father."

Watching him tentatively, she set down her water pot and brushed back a strand of ebony hair, tucking it under her veil. "I didn't expect to see you here, of all places. Have you decided to accept Abba's invitation after all?"

He narrowed his eyes at her. "No. I'm here to bring a caravan of goods. But I thought I would see him while I'm here."

Her gaze dropped. "I see."

She lowered the bucket into the well, but he put out his hand. "Please, allow me." He filled her water pot and heaved it onto his shoulder. "I'll follow you."

Her lips parted, but he couldn't tell if she was going to object, or if it was half a smile. She beckoned and headed toward the alley. "This way."

She wove through the back streets, glancing at him over her shoulder every so often as if afraid he'd get lost. They came to a row of quaint houses, and she knocked on one of the gates before opening the latch. She held the gate for him as he passed into the large courtyard enclosed by a stone wall. Several older women huddled around a fire, and men's voices echoed from one of the adjoining chambers. A cluster of young men standing at the far side of the courtyard burst into laughter, but fell quiet as he entered. His stomach knotted, and heat crept up his neck as he realized how it must look for him to enter carrying a woman's water pot.

"Malon." Andrew stepped away from them. "When did you arrive?"

One of Malon's eyebrows rose. *Just now.* But no, that wasn't the intent of his question. "Kish and I rode in this morning from Caesarea. We've brought a large caravan."

"Peter told us you weren't coming."

So Peter talked about him, then. The tips of Malon's ears burned. The water pot wasn't the only reason for the young men's stares. "I thought it would be rude not to stop in while I'm here."

Two children darted past, and he almost lost his hold on the water pot still balancing on his shoulder.

"Jacob and Jonas, what has Imah said to you about running? You nearly sent poor Brother Malon sprawling to the ground." Petronilla clicked her tongue and wiggled a finger at them. "You must learn to play nicely."

The two boys bowed identical heads. "Yes, Petronilla."

"Please apologize to Brother Malon."

"Sorry," they chimed in unison.

"Very well then, why don't you go get the marbles to play with? They're beneath my bed."

Their faces brightened as if the sun had come out from behind a cloud. They looked at each other, and then took off toward the chambers.

"Don't run, boys."

At her reminder, they slowed to an awkward half-walk, half-skip as they disappeared. This time, there was no mistaking her smile — as a summer's day. Just like Imah's.

With an apologetic look, Petronilla turned toward the

kitchen chamber. "If you'll set the pot in here, you won't need to hold it while you talk. I'll let Abba know you're here."

Malon set the pot down just inside the kitchen and refocused on Andrew. "Your brother visited us in Capernaum last week, but it's been a long while since I've seen you."

"I haven't been able to get away. There is much to do here, getting things established."

"Peter said there has been a lot of goings on."

"That's one way to put it." Andrew chuckled. "Things are certainly different since Pentecost. It has only been a few weeks, but it feels like ages. Come. Let me introduce you to the others. You're not the only young believer." Andrew touched his shoulder and guided him closer to the group of young men. "Brothers, a few of you may remember Malon. He's from Capernaum. His mother was healed by Jesus several years ago, and his family has been believers ever since."

Malon nodded a greeting. Most of the men looked older than himself, but he suspected they were still close to his age. Three had dark hair and dressed the part of typical Jews. The other had light hair, eyes as clear and blue as the skies, and high cheekbones.

"Welcome, Brother Malon." The light-haired one

offered a wide smile. "My name is Nicanor. Pleased to meet you."

A Greek name. That accounted for his fair appearance.

"Pleased to meet you as well."

One of the dark-headed Jews stretched out a hand, eyes sparkling above his smile. "I'm Stephen."

Malon clasped his hand and returned a grin.

"Well, if it isn't the young disciple." Peter's low tone interrupted them from across the courtyard. Beaming, the fisherman strode over and clasped Malon's arm. "We're glad you have come."

"I'm only here for a few days to sell the recent shipment from Caesarea."

"So I've heard." Peter glanced at his daughter, who had paused a few feet behind him. "You're welcome to stay as long as you like. We have a place for you to sleep. As you can see, you are not the only young lad in our ranks, and we've always got plenty to eat."

Malon scanned the courtyard and the people mingling there. "Do all these people live here?"

"Well, yes and no." Peter's eyes sparkled like the Galilee. "We live in a sort of commune. Some in this house, some in the surrounding houses. Everyone shares what they have, and the Lord blesses it."

Strange. They lived like family. Maybe that's why

Petronilla and the others had taken to calling everyone "brother". He wasn't sure he'd get used to that.

"We have a bit of time before supper from what I understand." When Peter turned to his daughter, she agreed, and he faced Malon again. "I have a few things to finish, but if I can steal you away from your peers here, would you keep me company while I work?"

Malon glanced at the others. Stephen smiled and made a shooing motion with his hand. "Very well. Anything I can do to help?"

Peter threw his head back and laughed. "I like that about you, Malon. A hard worker like your father. Come with me."

He followed the disciple to a chamber with a table, two chairs, and a set of shelves in the left corner. Several baskets occupied the shelves. A lamp stood at the center of the undecorated table, waiting to cast light on a wooden box and a couple scrolls beside it. His gaze lingered on the plain olive wood box. A fish made of two curved lines roughly carved into the lid.

"Go ahead. Open it." Peter motioned toward the box. "It's all right. I wanted to show you what's inside it."

Malon fingered the fish design. "A fisherman's box."

Peter grinned, a mischievous twinkle in his eye, but he said nothing.

Lifting the lid revealed a linen cloth folded ever so carefully inside the small wooden confine. "A napkin?"

"Not *a. The* napkin that covered Jesus face when they buried him. When I found it folded after he had risen, I took great care to pick it up, just as it was, and I keep it in there to remind me of the message, 'I am coming back'."

Malon stared at the linen, but it didn't hold the significance for him it must for Peter. He closed the lid and returned it to its spot on the table.

Peter lit the lamp, then walked around and took a seat before the scrolls. "You are accustomed to keeping ledgers, I suppose?"

"Yes. I help my father keep his books at the shop."

"I've kept a few from my fisherman days, but I admit they were not what they should be."

"What do you have to keep ledgers for now?"

"We all live here together, sharing everything in common. When someone sells their property, or if they make money somehow, they bring it to me to give into the common treasury, as we disciples did before Jesus was crucified. Keeping such ledgers is not my strong point. One of the many reasons I'd hoped you would join us." He winked.

Something about his humble and honest statement caused Malon to chuckle. Kish often deferred the record keeping to him as well. Malon pulled the other chair next to Peter's and sat. "What is the problem?"

Peter's finger slid down the lines. "There is a discrepancy somewhere, and I can't figure where. But the coins in the bag and the amount on the ledger do not match."

"When was the last time you balanced it?"

The disciple's sandy eyebrows scrunched in a wince. "Almost a month ago."

"Did it match then?"

"Yes."

"That's a start. Let's run though the most recent transactions and see if we can find the problem. What is this?" Malon pointed to a figure.

"We purchased meat from a local farmer. Here, we purchased cloth for the women, and this was grain."

"This is an increase of funds?"

"Yes, Barnabas sold his land and brought the entire sum and laid it at our feet, insisting we put it into the treasury."

"That's a large sum."

"Yes, it is. It was generous of him to contribute all of it. He kept not a single mite for himself."

Malon added the numbers in his head. "Are you sure these amounts you paid the farmer and the weaver are correct? Do you have a way to verify them?"

"Only my memory. I suppose we could go to them and see if the farmer's ledgers reflect the same."

With a shrug, he continued adding and subtracting. He wrote his calculations in a column next to Peter's. "Here it is. This was added wrong. When I recalculated it, the sum comes out."

Peter leaned forward and squinted at the number, then sat back with a sigh. "Lord, you know I need someone else to do this. I am but an uneducated fisherman."

A knock at the door interrupted them. An older man stood at the doorway. Graying hair covered his ears, and wrinkles creased around his eyes as he smiled. "Shalom, Peter. I hope I'm not disturbing you. Andrew said I would find you in here."

"Not at all. What can I do for you, Ananias?"

The man stepped into the room and pulled a moneybag out of his cloak. "My wife and I had a little land near Bethlehem. We sold it for a fair price of one hundred shekels, and we wish to give the whole amount to the treasury."

Malon's brows rose. What generous people.

Peter sat silent, regarding the man. Then he shook his head. "Ananias, why has Satan put it in your heart to lie to the Holy Ghost and keep back part of the price of the land?"

The man took a step back, apparently as stunned as Malon.

"Before you sold it, was it not yours? Even after? You could have given only a part of the price. Why then did you lie and say you had given it all? Why have you plotted this in your heart? You have not lied to men, but to God."

The man's eyes widened, and his face paled. He let out a groan and crumbled, the money skittering from the bag as he hit the stone floor.

Malon hastened to the man's side and knelt, pressing his fingers to the man's neck. No pulse. He was already cold. Malon's chest constricted, inhibiting his breathing, stealing his voice. Seconds passed before he could whisper, "He's dead."

Peter's face was stiff, and tears pooled in his eyes. "Go to the courtyard and bring the young men. We need to give Ananias a proper burial."

Tearing his eyes from the miserable expression on Ananias' face, Malon trotted into the courtyard. "Andrew?"

Stephen walked toward him, Nicanor following. "Is everything all right?"

"Peter needs a few men to..." What should he say? *Somebody come help me bury this dead man?* "Where is Andrew?"

"He's gone next door to speak with James and John," Stephen answered. "Does Peter need help with something?"

"Come." Malon led them to Peter's chamber.

Nicanor gasped when he spotted Ananias on the floor. "What has happened?"

Peter had been facing the wall, but he turned now. Tears streaked his tanned face. "He lied to God, and the Holy Spirit has smitten him. Take him out and bury him."

Eyes wide, the men obeyed. Malon helped them lift the body, and they carried it into another chamber. Petronilla brought linen cloths, and they took great care in preparing the body for burial. After several hours of tedious work, they finished. Stephen and Nicanor carried the bound body away.

Malon's hands trembled as the others left. "How did you know how much he sold the land for?" He couldn't bring himself to look at Peter. "Who told you the price of the land?"

"The Holy Ghost."

Frowning, he approached the disciple. "What do you mean?"

"When Ananias came into the room, I saw him making the transaction, and then dividing the money with his wife."

Malon swallowed hard. "He has a wife?"

"He does. I pray she will not be as foolish as he was, for here she comes."

He looked toward the door. No one was there. Doubt niggled at him, but after what had transpired, he wouldn't give in so quickly. He feared to. The thought of leaving, getting away from these strange events crossed his mind, but something held him there. He followed Peter into his chamber to resume his work on the scrolls. Malon's gaze fell to the coins still scattered across the floor. "What do you want done with the money?"

"For now, gather it up and leave it on the table."

He obeyed, dropping every coin into the pouch. He set the pouch on the corner of the table and resumed his seat before the scrolls.

"Abba, Sister Sapphira is here." Petronilla's forehead creased. Fear reflected in her eyes.

"Show her in, Pet."

Concern etched Petronilla's delicate features, but she obeyed and waved a hand behind her. A gray-headed woman approached the doorway.

"Sapphira, tell me, did you sell your land for one

hundred shekels?"

"Yes, for one hundred shekels." Her voice sounded pinched.

"Oh, Sapphira, how is it that you and your husband have agreed together to tempt the Spirit of the Lord?" Peter bit his lip, as if trying to hold back the tears trickling down his cheeks.

Voices in the corridor announced Stephen and Nicanor's return.

Bowing his head, Peter spoke. "Behold, the feet of them that have buried thy husband are at the door." His voice trembled. "And shall also carry you out."

Fear contorted her face. Then she too crumpled to the floor.

Peter looked away and placed a steadying hand on the wall. His body convulsed as he wept.

Chapter Thirteen

Supper was quiet, but Malon guessed it abnormal for the group surrounding him. The deaths of Ananias and Sapphira sobered everyone, and none felt to discuss it. In truth, Malon was relieved. Talk would have been awkward. Still, he couldn't take his eyes from Peter. He'd known the man all his life. Peter was Simon the fisherman, a good-natured workman who splashed him if he walked by without saying hello and always wore a grin as broad as the sea. But the Peter he'd witnessed today saw into the heart and life of Ananias and knew the things only God could know. This power didn't come from a common fisherman. No, as much as Malon didn't want to believe it, this power came from God.

So many questions needed asking, but with the somber mood, not to mention Petronilla hovering around serving the food, he couldn't bring himself to voice them.

He left at dawn and met Kish at the Cardo marketplace. The morning was busy, but as the sun rose higher, and with it the scalding temperatures, business dwindled. He and Kish sat beneath the canopy swatting at flies.

"Where did you lodge last night?" Kish asked. "You usually stay with me at my uncle's, but you didn't come."

"I found Andrew and Peter. I stayed with them."

Kish stiffened. "You know associating with the sons of Jonas is not the same as it used to be. They've become followers of that Nazarene, and the priests will expel you from the synagogue if you join them."

"Yes, Rabbi Ben-Elior made it quite clear." Best not to talk about what he'd seen the night before, though he was bursting to tell someone. He'd wait and give his report to Abba as he'd promised.

"I've been meaning to speak with your father on this matter. I fear he is endangering our business by associating with these disciples and claiming to be one of Jesus' followers. You too. If the both of you continue this way, our business will be ruined, and you will take me and my family down with you."

Malon leaned forward and folded his hands in front of him. "What are you saying?"

"I have served your family for many years, and I have never butted into your affairs. What you believe is your business, but when you start touting it to the high priests, it becomes mine."

"Are you implying we're purposefully damaging our business and reputation? Do you think we want to lose the income from the Pharisees?"

"Of course not. I just want—or need—you to realize your actions in this don't only affect you and your income. They may destroy mine."

*****

"Abba? Imah? Are you here?" Malon paused in the empty courtyard. Silence. Not even a mouse or cricket chirped.

The scent of fresh bread teased his nostrils, and the door to the bedchamber stood ajar.

Maybe they've gone to Savta's house. His pulse began pounding in his ears, despite his attempts to explain their absence. His stomach twisted. His fears surfaced. Had Barabbas returned?

He searched the house, almost relieved to find it as empty as it sounded. At least he didn't discover them massacred by the ruthless villain. Still, every nerve in his body tingled, and his thoughts grew more and more difficult to control.

Savta's. Go to Savta's house. They must be there.

It wasn't uncommon for the family to visit his grandmother, and they hadn't seen her since Topaz's dedication. She was too old to visit their home, so surely Abba had taken them to see her.

With his heart still pounding against his ribcage, he hurried through the streets. The sun sank low beyond the stone houses. Just the time of day when Barabbas liked to make his appearance. Dust, aroused by his sprint, clung to his sticky palms. He never should have consented to leave for so long. Kish could have handled the caravan, and he would have been here to help Abba keep Imah and Topaz safe.

Please, Adonai.

He brushed off his hands before knocking on Savta's gate. It cracked open, and a woman's round face with a dark skeptical glare peeked through. "Auntie Tzivyah, are Abba and Imah here?"

The skepticism melted, replaced by a doting smile. "Yes, they're here."

A stagnant breath left his lungs. *Praise God.*

She swung open the door and ushered him inside. "Come in. I didn't know you had returned. You must be hungry. How was your journey? Look who's here, everyone," she called as they entered the small courtyard.

Savta hobbled out of house with Abba and Imah following. "Malon, come give your old grandmother a hug."

He wrapped his arms around Savta's frail frame while meeting his father's gaze. "I panicked when you weren't home. I thought harm had befallen while I was gone."

Abba pressed his lips together and shrugged. "I'm sorry. I didn't expect you yet, so I gave no thought to it."

"Where is Topaz?" He eyed Imah's empty arms.

"She's inside the house. Your uncle was holding her near the hearth, but he was too afraid to stand or walk with her, so we left him sitting there when Tzivyah called out."

Malon smiled. He knew the feeling. The babe seemed as if she would break if you moved your arms in the wrong way. The thought of dropping her petrified him. She might shatter like a porcelain relic.

He hugged his mother, lingering an extra moment before letting her go. He'd only gotten her back three years ago; he wasn't about to lose her again. "Well, I think Uncle Tiltan has had his turn. I want to hold my sister."

He led the way into the house. Stools, gathered from every part of the house, crowded the hearth, and it emitted a glow as warm as the love in each eye. Malon extended his arms toward his uncle with a wink. "Surrender the babe, and you may keep your life."

Tiltan lifted his chin. "You forget, nephew, Topaz is my baby sister."

"Not this Topaz. This one's mine." He jabbed a finger into his uncle's shoulder. With their slight age differences, Tiltan felt more like an older brother than an uncle. They spent most of their time together in jest and sport.

Scooping the babe in his arms, he bounced her a few times as he'd seen his mother do. "Shalom, beautiful. Did you miss me while I was gone?" he cooed.

Her baby lips parted in a yawn, and then settled into a satisfied smile as she nestled against his chest. Warmth spread through him like honey over Savta's homemade bread. He settled on a bench next to Abba and stared down at her. His awe seemed to rest over everyone in the room, the only sound the crackling fire in the stone hearth.

"How was your trip?" Abba asked.

"Enlightening," he replied without taking his gaze from Topaz. "And at the same time, terrifying."

Abba's brows creased, exposing deep wrinkles between his eyes. "What do you mean?"

"The business part went well."

"Of course." Abba shrugged. "We can discuss it at the

shop tomorrow with Kish. Did you see Simon and Andrew?"

"I did, and I saw much more."

All eyes locked on him, so he took a deep breath. "To be honest, I don't know what to make of all I saw. I arrived in Jerusalem with Kish, and after we set up, I went looking for the disciples. Peter's daughter came to the well and led me to where they reside. They live together on one street and have all things in common. A few of them have even sold land and given all the money into the treasury. They share all they have equally, with whoever has need, as if they're one big family. They even call each other brother and sister."

Imah nodded, and her big brown eyes urged him to continue.

"Lots of young men have joined the believers in Jerusalem. I met several while I was there, but they are not all Jews. Some are Greeks."

"Simon said Gentiles, and even Samaritans, have believed on Jesus," Abba said.

"Peter needed assistance with his money ledgers, and since I was experienced in the keeping of them, he asked me to help. As I did, a man came in and told Peter he'd sold a piece of land for so much and wanted to give the entire amount into the treasury. Then Peter asked him why he lied about the matter. Peter told him he could have kept back a portion of the money if he wished, but when he lied and said he gave it all, he lied to God rather than to man. Then the man fell over dead."

"Dead?" A hoarse voice screeched at his right.

He shifted. "Yes, Savta. I don't know what happened. I can only suppose God struck him dead right on the spot."

"It is a terrible sin to lie. We know this from the law of Moses." Abba shook his head. "To lie to God, how serious that is."

"About three hours later, the man's wife came in and repeated his lie. She too fell down dead in the same spot."

Imah gasped.

Uncle Tiltan leaned forward and braced his elbows on his knees, his hands folded under his chin. "Unbelievable, and Peter didn't touch them?"

"No. He was standing next to me, across the room from where they stood in the threshold."

"How did Simon know the price of the land?" Abba lifted a hand to stroke his beard.

"I asked the same question. He said the Holy Spirit told him. He saw them standing in their house, planning this together. He heard their words, though he wasn't there."

Abba stood and paced to the other side of the room,

still rubbing his beard. "Then it is true. Jesus is alive." He turned to Malon. "He must be. We know the sign of the Messiah is to know the secrets of the heart. Only God can know that. So if he has resurrected, and has sent His spirit upon them as Simon says, then the same signs that He did would be shown forth in the disciples. If what you say really happened, then they are."

Topaz wiggled, and Malon shifted her. It was true. Jesus had known their family's situation without having met them before. He'd known of Imah's sickness, of Abba's dreams, even when no one else did. What Peter had known and done with Ananias and Sapphira was the same. Abba was right. Only God could know these things, so it had to be a sign of God. A vindication that what they said was the truth.

As they walked home, Malon's heart suddenly grew wings and soared into the stars above their heads. All doubt disappeared and, with it, the cloud of sorrow that had followed him for weeks.

Jesus is the Messiah. And he is alive.

Chapter Fourteen

I haven't forgotten.

Malon's hands shook as he tore the paper from the arrow nailing it to the shop door. The red ink gleamed as if...was it written with *blood?* Fear gouged his chest. What had Vitalis told him about the shrew?

Don't let his tactics paralyze you.

It could only be from Barabbas. No one else would leave such a note. The real question — Malon's real fear — was why had he not come already? Why deliver such a note without wreaking havoc like he usually did?

One thing was certain, as much as he wanted to, no way could he return to Jerusalem. Not for any length of time, anyway. There would be the caravans, but he'd avoid those if possible.

He strode into the shop and slapped the note on the

table. Abba wouldn't be in for another hour, but he'd show him when he arrived.

"Shalom, Malon." Kish poked his head inside. "I'm on my way to Noah's farm to collect the olive oil for next week's caravan."

"Very well." Malon nodded. "I will be around to help transfer the load when you get back. I'm finishing the lists. Do you think we can sell more of Jakka's wool? I'm considering increasing our order."

"There is a lot of wool in the Cardo, but ours sold well last time. I think the buyers liked the finer quality."

"True. Perhaps I will consult Abba before making the decision."

Kish shrugged and waved. "I will be back before midday."

Malon refocused on the list.

Dates, wool, olive oil, dried fish, baskets, Savta's salve.

What else would be profitable in Jerusalem? He added almonds and sat back with a sigh. His gaze fell upon Barabbas's note. How was he supposed to focus with his threat lurking?

Abba entered and smiled. "You do not know how much I love having you here. Running this business is so much easier since I have you to rely on." He stopped short. "What's wrong?"

With a painful swallow, Malon pointed to the note. "I found this. Someone shot our door with an arrow, and this note was attached."

Abba grasped the paper and scanned the line. His forehead creased. "Barabbas?"

"Must be."

"I still don't understand how he got out of the colony alive." His father's jaw clenched. "The man is invincible."

"Abba, I don't think I should be leaving on any caravans. We'll have to send Kish, but we need both of us here in case Barabbas retaliates. No telling what he will do. The shop, Imah, and Topaz...we can't afford to risk it."

"You're right." Abba let out a sigh. "We will have to send Kish, but he'll need help. We can pair him with Caleb, but then we would only have the one caravan running, which is hardly enough to supply Herodium, much less Jerusalem, and our revenue from the coast cities would diminish."

"Barabbas will be more angry and vengeful than ever. We'll have to pray Adonai will bless what we can manage. We can condense the Herodium trips, as well as Jerusalem, and then Caleb and Kish can work together on the large loads." Malon stood. "I'm going out to tend the displays. Would you care to look over my lists and make any corrections? I'm nearly done with the Jerusalem train."

Abba nodded as Malon walked past him and out the door. The Judean sun shone bright as he stepped into the fresh air. The briny Sea of Galilee sent a fresh tang through the air, hampered by smell of fish brought in that morning. Nearer, the scent of fresh baked bread wafted from the bakery across the market.

A couple of Roman soldiers stopped to look at the displays. He forced a smile and somehow managed to be courteous. Their purchases justified the effort.

He'd only come to like one Roman soldier. Tertius Dexius Vitalis. The centurion. Actually, it might be worth paying him a visit. If he told him of Barabbas's note, maybe he'd have further philosophical advice on how to kill this shrew. For certain this time.

As soon as they closed up shop, Malon headed toward the garrison. He'd miss supper, but he was too nervous to eat. Talking things over with the centurion would bring relief. He hoped. A cool breeze soothed his arms as he strode down the lane. The shadows cast by the basalt stone houses on either side added to his gloom. Barabbas could be lurking behind any of these structures, or in the alleys. Breathing became easier when the garrison came into view.

"I'm here to see Centurion Vitalis," he told the guard.

"The centurion is not here."

"Not here? Where is he?"

The guard rolled his eyes, as if explaining something to a Jew degraded him. "At home, I'd expect. Isn't that were most people go when they're off duty?"

Stifling his irritation over the guard's attitude, Malon thanked him and started toward the centurion's villa. One of the nicest houses in the village, everyone knew where it was.

Large eagles carved out of marble stood at the edge of his property. A dirt road slithered from the main street to the front of the villa. Tall, slim trees lined each side. Malon took in an awed breath. What it would be like to call such a place "home"?

He was about halfway up the lane, when someone exited the house and walked toward him. It looked like a Jew. Why would another Jew be at the centurion's house?

As the figure drew closer, he recognized the sturdy gait and sandy hair that whipped in the breeze. "Peter?"

The man lifted a hand. "Hello, Malon. What brings you to the centurion's house?"

"I was going to ask the same of you."

A grin plastered Peter's face. "Vitalis asked me to pay him a visit. He wanted to know what had become of Jesus. I was only too happy to enlighten him." Peter regarded Malon for a moment with a twinkle in his eye. "So, my young friend, have you decided whether or not to believe me?"

"That Vitalis sent for you?"

"No, about Jesus."

Malon bit his lip. "You mean that he truly is the Messiah, that he has resurrected, and that he has sent his spirit to live inside you?"

Peter nodded, still watching him.

"It is as my father said. If Jesus is alive, and if his spirit is living in you, then you will do the same works Jesus did. And you are. I've known you all my life, and I know the power you now possess is not your own. I have no choice but to believe it came from God. In this, I know you speak the truth."

"Then you believe the Messiah is alive."

"Yes, he has to be."

"Then I have something else to ask you, Malon Ben-Tyrus." Peter stepped closer, the twinkle in his eye fading. Instead, it seemed the man could gaze into his very soul. "Are you called to be one of his disciples?"

For a moment, Malon didn't know how to respond. He hadn't considered that an option since Jesus had died. But Jesus was alive. That changed things.

"Does your heart still hear the Master's call?" Peter asked again.

Taking a deep breath, Malon dared to say the words his heart feared. "I hear it louder now than before." This admission eased his raging mind, but an ache formed in his ribcage.

"Then join us. Help me spread the good news to all the cities in Israel."

What about my family? What about the business? Barabbas?

His heart pounded. No way could he leave. Not now. "I cannot go with you, Peter. My family needs me."

Peter regarded him, his eyes searching Malon's face. "You say you believe, but you refuse to act upon your faith."

"It's not so simple." Irritation seethed inside him, twisting his stomach into a knot. "I have the worst outlaw in the land out to kill me and my family, and you want me to leave them to come to Jerusalem?"

The disciple shook his head. "So much fear in your eyes. Fear is the enemy of faith. Put your trust in the Lord, obey Him, and He will take care of you." Peter reached out and squeezed Malon's shoulder. "I will pray for you."

Malon frowned as the disciple walked away. The sick feeling in his gut intensified. What was he supposed to do? He believed Peter. He believed Jesus. He also believed Barabbas.

I have not forgotten.

For now, Peter and Jesus would have to wait. One problem at a time. After he'd taken care of Barabbas, then he could sort everything out.

With a sigh, he continued toward Vitalis' house. He knocked at the courtyard gate, and a servant peeked out.

"Malon Ben-Tyrus here to see the centurion, please."

The servant opened the gate and waved him inside. He paused in the courtyard and waited for the servant to fetch his master. Tapestries and statues of the Roman fashion graced the elegant house. Laughter and happy chatter wafted from inside. Vitalis appeared, wearing a grin big enough to match his house. "Malon, to what do I owe this visit?"

"Shalom, Centurion. I hope I am not interrupting."

"No. What can I do for you?"

"I'm in need of friendly counsel if you can spare a moment."

The centurion glanced behind him at the bustling servants, and then nodded toward the gate. "Let's take a stroll in my vineyard."

Falling into pace beside him, Malon took in the hillside. Positioned on top of a knoll, with vineyards and olive trees surrounding it like loyal subjects protecting their monarch, the villa reigned the countryside. Green vines stood out against dark earth, and the soft jade of olive leaves reached toward the turquoise sky. He inhaled and allowed the freshness of the countryside to seep into his being. Exactly what he needed to clear his thoughts.

When they were a safe distance from the house, Vitalis clasped his hands behind his back. "So, what is it you wanted to speak with me about?"

Malon cleared his throat. Where to begin? "The shrew evaded our trap. He is more angry now than ever."

The centurion's lips pressed into a thin line. He walked several paces before asking, "Do you know where he is?"

"No, but he must be close by. The night of the fire, we heard him cry out that he would stop at nothing to kill me. We haven't heard or seen anything else until today. I found an arrow shot into our door with this note."

He pulled the paper from his tunic and handed it to Vitalis, who read the phrase with a mere glance. "How could he have survived?"

"I hardly got through the flames, and everything came crashing down behind me. I can't work out how he did, but obviously…"

"Either that, or someone else is carrying out his hostilities."

Doubtful, but a possibility — a possibility he hadn't

considered. "What can we do?"

"Besides wait?" Vitalis watched him from the corner of his eye as he strode along the rows. "I think you'd better pray. You're a Jew, are you not?"

"I am. Though lately, it seems the Lord has not heard my prayers."

"Maybe you can get Peter to pray for you."

"He said he would, but he and I are at a difference of opinions. He wants me to go with him to Jerusalem, but I can't leave with all this danger."

They approached the stables and paused where a servant worked with a bay stallion. Vitalis watched with warmth in his eyes and jutted his chin toward them. "You see the stallion? The servant guides him, and when he obeys, his path is clear and smooth. When he doesn't obey, his feet stumble, and the servant cracks the whip to drive him into step."

Malon shifted and leaned against the fence.

"I seem to recall a story in your Torah somewhat similar. A man who didn't want to do what God asked of him. He made excuses and ran the opposite direction. God caused evil things to happen to him in order to bring him to obedience."

"Jonah."

"Yes, that was it." Vitalis turned his gaze from the

stallion and let it rest upon Malon. "Are you a Jonah, young friend?"

The question stung as much as the whip that lashed the stallion's flank. Was he rebelling as Jonah had? No. Rebellion didn't keep him from joining Peter. But duty. A need to protect his family. Circumstances beyond his control. Wasn't it?

"I am not a Jonah."

"Then perhaps you are a Job. Is that not in your Torah as well?"

"Yes, Job was a righteous man, but God allowed him to be tested to prove his trust and loyalty to God."

Trust. And loyalty. If these were the tests HaShem had for him, was he failing?

"Fear is the enemy of faith, Malon. Put your trust in the Lord, obey Him, and He will take care of you."

Apparently, Peter thought so.

"Do you think it would be right for me to leave my family now? Surely, as a man of duty, you understand why I feel I cannot."

Vitalis nodded. "I understand, but must you leave your family to do what God requires of you?" He placed a hand on Malon's shoulder. "You asked for my advice, and I will give it. Go to Peter and find out what you must do, lest a worse curse come upon you. God is also bound by

duty, and He will take care of your family while you seek
His will."

Chapter Fifteen

Malon prayed he was making the right decision, inhaled a deep breath, and rapped on the gate, marveling that he could recall the twists and turns to the right house. He'd only followed Petronilla here once, and the disciples' abode was deep in the quarter.

"Who's there?" a familiar voice called from inside.

"Petronilla? It's Malon."

"Malon?"

"Malon Ben-Tyrus."

The gate swung open wide, revealing her puzzled expression. "You seem to have a talent for showing up directly after it has been sworn we won't see a hint of you."

He winced. Not more gossip. "Is your father here?"

She moved aside so he could enter, and he stepped out

of the street. The gate creaked as she shut it behind him. "Abba, look who has arrived."

Peter turned and lifted a hand to stroke his tangled beard. "Well, you've come."

"I don't know how long I can stay, but I must know. I believe your words. I know Jesus is the Messiah, and I want to do His will. What must I do?"

The edges of Peter's mouth lifted amidst his scruffy beard, and his eyes softened. "Then I give you the same answer I give to all those who ask. Repent and be baptized in the name of Jesus Christ, and you shall receive the gift of the Holy Ghost."

"I am a Jew, and I have followed the commandments from birth. How am I to repent?"

"You have followed the traditions of the scribes and Pharisees from birth, but the Lord's commandments are far above the traditions of men. For where the scribes say, 'an eye for an eye and a tooth for a tooth', Christ says 'if any man strike you, turn to him the other cheek as well.' He said also, 'if a man would compel you to go a mile, go with him two.'"

Malon took a step back. He hadn't expected this when he imagined following the Messiah. "You mean, if a Roman soldier compels me to carry his pack, I must carry it twice as far? I thought the Messiah was coming to free us from Roman rule, not oppress us further."

Peter's head tilted, and that iron gaze locked in. "Tell me, what would set you free? Bitterness and anger toward the Romans, or possessing the power to forgive? The power to serve them despite their cruelty?"

What a power that would be. Right now, Malon couldn't imagine himself possessing such strength. He recalled the last mile that he walked with Gallus. Forced servitude, even with stripes on his back. And what of Barabbas? Should he allow him to strike him and his family over and over, turning the other cheek? The Master asked much more than he'd ever imagined.

"Malon, there is a slavery much greater than the oppression of Rome or the Pharisees or even Barabbas. Which is the greater slave? Your body or your soul?"

Malon looked away and clenched his jaw. Which indeed? Pressure from the Romans, and even more so from Barabbas, weighed heavily on him. A day didn't pass that he wondered what treachery would be inflicted upon him next. Yet down inside him was something stronger, heavier, so intense at times he could hardly breathe. His soul was suffocating, choked by fear, pride, and hatred. He'd wanted freedom, but what good would freedom do him if his heart didn't change? Nausea swarmed his stomach. He closed his eyes. He'd sunk to the same level as Gallus. In his anger and hatred, he'd become like him.

"I want what you have, Peter. I want the power to forgive."

"Are you certain? This is not a decision to make lightly. Public baptism in the name of Jesus Christ will brand you. They will expel you from your synagogue and persecute you."

"Freedom comes with a price, and if what Jesus endured on the cross was for me, then this sacrifice is nothing in comparison."

"Very well then, let's find a pool."

*****

Clouds of dust hovered over the streets, but Malon's mouth was dry for another reason. As they neared the Pool of Siloam, a hundred reasons to change his mind pelted him. What would Abba say when he heard? Would he be glad, or angry he'd created such detriment for their business? The Pool of Siloam lay within sight of the Temple Mount, and amidst the bustling section of the Lower City. No telling who might be standing around to see his baptism.

Andrew, Stephen, Nicanor, and the other disciples gathered as Peter waded down the steps and into the pool.

He looked to Malon with a wide grin and beckoned him with one hand, the other palm resting on the water's surface.

Heart pounding, Malon stepped down into the cool water. Liquid enveloped his ankles and licked at the hem of his robe. He blinked away the thoughts of who might be observing, and pressed his way toward Peter. The sun beamed down in heat waves as the disciple placed a hand on the back of Malon's neck and held onto his forearm with the other.

"I have been commissioned by Jesus Christ to go into all the world preaching the gospel and baptizing them in the name of the Father, Son, and Holy Spirit. So today, Malon Ben-Tyrus, upon the confession of your faith and your sincere repentance, I now fulfill my commission and baptize you in the name of our Lord Jesus Christ."

Malon allowed himself to dip backward. The water encased him. As he emerged, droplets ran down his face, as if cleansing away every speck of impurity. The pool had saturated his clothes and hair, and somehow, his soul. It seemed every mark, every work of the past had been stripped away and swirled behind him as he escaped to dry land. Stephen held out a hand to steady him when he ascended the slick stairs, water sloshed from his sandals when he reached the top.

Andrew wrapped his arms around Malon's shoulders in a brotherly embrace. "Mozel tov, Malon. You're a new man."

Malon smiled. He certainly felt like a new man, as if his heart had grown wings and could soar like an eagle above the city, out of reach of Barabbas and all his troubles. Then his eyes locked with a man standing in the street. The feeling vanished.

Kish's jaw tightened. His eyes narrowed to slits. He stood for what seemed like years, his only movement the slight shake of his head. Then he disappeared into the crowd.

*****

Malon arrived at the Cardo at sunrise. He and Kish had a multitude of goods to sell before they returned to Capernaum. He'd told Abba he needed to go with Kish, despite Barabbas's threats, and he didn't regret it. A strange peace rested over him, unlike he'd ever experienced. He no longer feared what Barabbas might do in his absence. He didn't worry about his family, and he was not concerned about the day's commerce. The Almighty's hand was upon him, and all would be well.

He arranged their goods in their assigned block and

waited for Kish. The produce he set beneath the canopy, and the stable goods closer to the street. Already the city was coming to life as women emerged carrying baskets and pots on their heads. Soon, customers began stopping by his booth, and by the time the sun shone high above the pavilion, he'd sold a good portion of their inventory. Perhaps the smile on his face and the joy bubbling inside him inclined people to buy from him.

A grumble emanated from his stomach. Must be time for the midday meal. Frowning, he glanced around. Where was Kish? He was supposed to have arrived hours ago. He scanned the marketplace, his frown deepening. Merchants called out to a rich woman on a litter. One seller flung a long strip of expensive fabric toward her, but one of the servants tripped over it and stumbled. The litter lurched, nearly tossing the lady. Malon had to bite his tongue to keep from laughing at the horror on the merchant's face. The inspector evaluated booths and prices as he passed, but Kish was nowhere to be seen.

"Can you take a break for something to eat?"

Malon met Stephen's grin. "Nice of you to join me. I was beginning to think I'd have to eat alone."

Stephen held up a basket. "Petronilla packed us bread and cheese. If you'll lend some of your dates for dessert, I think we'll be just fine."

"Thoughtful of her," Malon mumbled. Why did it make him feel so odd? It wasn't abnormal for her to send him food…was it? "But we'll have to eat here. Without Kish, I can't leave our booth."

"Suits me." Stephen gave a shrug. "I rather enjoy watching people in the marketplace."

Malon chuckled. Some people could certainly provide amusement. He motioned to a barrel for Stephen and turned over a crate for himself.

Stephen sat and unwrapped the bread and cheese. When he looked up, Malon nodded and bowed his head.

"Lord, we thank You for this food we are about to partake of," Stephen began. "You have provided for all our needs, and we're grateful. We are also grateful, Lord, for the truth You have revealed to our young brother Malon. I pray You would continue to bless him, fill him with Your Spirit, lead him, and direct his path. We ask it in the name of Jesus Christ, and we'll give You all the glory and honor forever and ever, amen."

When Malon opened his eyes, he pressed his lips into a smile. "Thank you."

Stephen handed him a hunk of bread and cheese. "How long before your other worker returns?"

"I don't know. He was supposed to be here early this morning, but I've not seen or heard from him." Malon took a bite and chewed. What would have kept Kish from work? The image of the man's face the night before as he witnessed his baptism surfaced. "I wonder—"

"Wonder what?" Stephen quirked a brow.

"If my help may have abandoned me."

"Why would he? Hasn't he worked with your family for a long time?"

"Yes, he has been my father's apprentice for more than ten years, but he hasn't taken too kindly to my acceptance of Jesus. He begged me not to make public my beliefs. Last night, he was amongst the crowd as Peter baptized me."

Stephen tore his bread in half and stacked slices of cheese in between. "It wouldn't be the first time something like that happened. Peter warned you that you may be persecuted."

"He was a partner in the company, so I don't think he can just leave. I'm not sure what we'll do."

They fell silent for a moment, staring at the passersby. Stephen leaned forward and rested his arms on his knees. "Malon, can I ask you a strange question?"

"Um, I suppose so."

"Your home…is it a large villa with a courtyard?"

"Yes."

"Your parent's bedchamber…is it the room in the east corner of the courtyard?"

Malon's eyebrows lowered. "It is. Why?"

"Your shop is on the northeast corner of the square, across from the custom's booth."

How strange. "How do you know this? Have you seen us in Capernaum?"

Stephen shook his head. "Last night, I had a dream, and I believe it may have been sent by the Holy Spirit."

Biting his lip, Malon nodded. "Go on."

"I saw you and your family. A tainted man with few teeth was very wroth with you. He came and set fire to your house and shop."

A lump formed in Malon's throat. "Barabbas." He stood and paced around the booth. "What should I do?"

"Malon." Stephen waited for him to meet his eyes. "Your mother and sister didn't make it out alive."

Malon's heart stopped. "What?"

"They were trapped inside the bedchamber."

"Oh, God." He gripped his hair and pressed his eyes closed. "I have to reach them."

"You don't have much time. In the dream, the night your villa burned, the moon was like a splinter in the hand of darkness."

"Without Kish here, I can't leave the booth. I'd have to pack everything and take it all back, and it would take too much time."

"Don't worry. Nicanor and I will take care of the booth."

Pressing his lips together, Malon dipped his head. A poor substitute for the thanks he couldn't voice.

"You're welcome. Now go." Stephen waved him away with a flick of his hand. "Godspeed, my brother."

Chapter Sixteen

Malon dug his heels into the horse's flank, spurring him faster across the barren plain. He'd borrowed a horse from the Jerusalem stable and switched mounts once already at Sebastia, but it would still be hours before he reached Capernaum. He prayed he could make it by nightfall. Crossing the 120 miles between the Holy City and his hometown was difficult on camels, and not much better on a horse. He'd been running the animal as fast as the roads allowed, but the rough and barren land between here and Nazareth slowed the stallion's gait as he navigated rocks and uneven ground. The heat of the sun made moments pass like years. Would he ever reach his family?

Despite the urgency driving him forward, an absence of the paralyzing fear that usually accompanied thoughts of Barabbas surprised Malon. The out-of-control feeling didn't surface. Most surprising, he didn't feel the anger he harbored toward the outlaw. Instead, a power and confidence rested near his heart and emanated through his chest, giving his limbs strength and purpose.

The sun sank low as he rode into Nazareth. The travel from here would be easier, but the threads of time holding the lives of his family were growing thin. As the sun faded, the moon appeared in a sliver above the horizon, glowing an eerie red and shining brighter with each moment.

He clicked his tongue and leaned forward, but the rented horse struggled. The beast's sides heaved each breath. "Please, boy, my family's lives depend upon us."

Do they really? Or do their lives depend upon the Lord?

Malon repented of the thought. "Forgive me, Adonai. I am depending on You. Please protect my family, and help me to get there in time."

His mind traveled faster than his body, and he imagined Barabbas sneaking around the city with torches illuminating his ugly face. "Please, Lord. And help me know what to do when I arrive."

As he galloped from behind the last set of crags, the Capernaum gates loomed ahead, and his heart sank. He came to a skidding halt. Closed and locked. Eight-foot tall cedar boards with iron hinges stood between him and his family.

He dropped from horseback to the ground and stared up at them. "Hello? Anyone there?" No guard appeared. He pounded the gate. "Please open the gate!"

Nothing. Where were the guards? Had they fallen asleep? Left their post? He rested his head against the stout wood. His breath huffed against it and back in his face. "HaShem, You have sent me here. You gave Stephen the dream. Won't You open the gate?"

Seek and ye shall find. Ask and it shall be given. Knock, and the door will be answered unto you.

He pounded on the gates once more, but this time, they budged. Placing both palms against them, he pushed. The great oak doors creaked, opening about a foot. Just enough for him to squeeze through.

Thank You, Lord.

Breaking into a run, he entered the marketplace. Everything was still, the shop unscathed. He dashed toward the house, but his sides seized in such pain, he had to stop. Groaning, he clutched them and took a few deep breaths. Then gritting his teeth, he pressed forward as fast as he could, but managed little more than stumbling.

When at last he came close enough to make out the familiar engraving of a star on the wooden door, he allowed a pause. The vines still dangled across the threshold, gently swinging in the night breeze, and all was still. He'd made it. He leaned against the stone wall enclosing the courtyard and breathed. He closed his eyes, thanking God for His protection.

When he opened his eyes again, he spotted movement slinking down the lane. Encroaching like a hoard of spiders, several men in dirty robes crept toward the gate, holding unlit torches. Two limbered over the wall, but a third stood before the gate. He fiddled with the latch, making hardly a sound, and opened it. He signaled to the remaining men, who faded into the shadows. Then he slipped inside.

Barabbas. Malon's pulse thundered. What should he do? He had no weapon, and Abba would be sleeping. How would he rouse him in time?

Adonai, help me. Tell me what to do.

Not wasting another moment, he strode forward and pushed open the gate. The dark figure whirled around at the creak.

"Barabbas, stop."

The villain smiled, his scant yellow teeth the only distinguishable feature in the darkness. "Well, well, if it isn't the young hero. How did you get back from Jerusalem so quickly?"

"How did you make it out of the colony fire alive?"

With an odd growl, Barabbas lurched to the dim lamp burning in the middle of the courtyard and lit his torch. Light illuminated his face and stole Malon's breath. His features were no longer as Malon remembered. Instead, they resembled a melted candle, scarred and burned beyond recognition, with eyebrows singed away and flesh bubbled and rough.

"If you'd have seen me in the daylight, you wouldn't have recognized me." Barabbas's tone shivered cold and low. "You're the one responsible for this."

The sight sickened Malon's stomach. He'd meant to kill Barabbas then, but he'd failed. He'd caused the man great pain and suffering. Still, he'd done it to protect his family.

"You look so surprised." Barabbas laughed, but his black eyes held no humor. "After you escaped the flames, I hid inside the cistern. The fire burned all around me, and the heat scorched my face and arms, but I survived. Since then, I have lived for this night. To cause you the same pain and suffering you have caused me."

"I'm sorry," Malon choked.

Barabbas frowned.

"I was defending my family. But I am sorry to see you suffer." Had he done the wrong thing then? He'd imagined

Barabbas as a monster, a man beyond human feeling, but seeing his wounded face, his pain-filled scars, brought his humanity to light with a force that lanced deep.

"You're sorry? Do you think that helps? Do you think it will save your sorry life and deter me from taking my revenge?"

Those words should have struck fear. Instead, Malon melted in compassion, and tears streamed down his face. Taking a deep breath, he forced out the words lodged in his throat. "I know my apology means nothing to you in light of your pain, and you have every reason to feel the way you do. I don't blame you for wanting to kill me, but please spare my family. Do whatever you want to me, but let them go. They're innocent."

Something flickered on Barabbas's expression, but his sneer soon chased it away. He snapped his fingers, and his men emerged from the shadows and gripped Malon's arms. One pressed a knife to his throat.

Barabbas crept toward him, raising the torch, his face tight and intent. He came so close, the heat from the torch singed Malon's tunic. The fabric near his throat began smoking, and the stench of the burning wool seared his nostrils.

"I'll start with you," Barabbas hissed. "If my revenge isn't satisfied by the time you give up the ghost, I'll move on to your family."

Malon struggled not to panic at the heat and pain intensifying on his chest. He looked Barabbas in the eye and imagined him trapped inside the cistern at the leper colony, without as much as a prayer, since he didn't have a God to pray to. The tears in his eyes were as hot and stinging as the torch at his breast, and his heart felt it too.

Barabbas's gaze faltered, and he stepped back. He growled, and then looked up again. "Hold up his hands."

His men raised Malon's hands and extended them toward Barabbas. The outlaw no longer met Malon's eyes. He focused, instead, on the torch as he wafted it beneath Malon's left palm. The flame seared the tender skin. Malon clamped his mouth shut as scream clawed up his throat, and his nose wrinkled at the odor of burning flesh.

"Did you smell your own skin burning as you huddled inside the cistern?" The steadiness in his own voice surprised Malon.

Barabbas squinted, and he moved the torch from Malon's palm, to his wrist.

Oh, the pain. Lord, keep me strong. How did Barabbas keep from going completely mad? "I, at least, have the advantage of fresh air. You must have been suffocating from the smoke with the colony burning around you. How did you breathe?"

With a roar, Barabbas dropped the torch and clasped both hands around Malon's throat. The rasping breaths didn't help. Malon's vision swam. He flailed panicky hands until the man thrust him against the courtyard wall. He hit hard, but had no breath to be knocked from him on impact. He collapsed on the stone floor, wheezing as he struggled to his hands and knees.

Barabbas snatched a sword from one of his men and flung it in front of him. "Pick it up," he growled.

Heat still gnawed the flesh on Malon's left palm, but he ignored it and pushed to his feet.

"Pick it up." Barabbas drew his sword and crouched in a defensive position.

"I don't want to fight. I've already caused you enough pain."

Barabbas's face reddened. "Go get the baby."

Alarm ripped through Malon. He spun to the left.

A rouge scampered toward his parent's bedchamber, sword in hand. A shriek, then commotion. Finally, the man emerged, clutching Topaz clumsily in his free arm, followed by Imah's wails.

The man stood next to Barabbas, awaiting further orders.

"Pick up the sword, scum."

Malon bent and grasped it in his right hand, not

taking his eyes off his enemy. "We don't have to do this. You have me. I'm your willing prisoner."

Barabbas's eyes flashed, and he lunged. Instinct seized him, and Malon's sword thwarted the advance. Their blades locked.

The outlaw's furious strength easily overpowered Malon's battered body, and the blade started to slip toward his throat. He ducked, deflecting the blade and spinning out of Barabbas's reach.

Adonai, help me. I don't want to kill him, but I have to protect my sister.

His enemy panted as he advanced again. He delivered several hard blows, but displayed little strategy, simply flinging his weapon as hard as he could, letting it fall where it would. Malon dodged them, leading the spar away from Topaz and his parent's bedchamber.

"Malon!" Abba emerged from the bedchamber, blood trickling down his temple. Imah clung to his arm.

Thwack.

Pain reverberated through Malon's head as Barabbas's sword hilt connected with his skull. His ears squealed, and red liquid dripped into his eyes. Stumbling, he fell to the floor, his burned palm colliding with the stones.

"Get up!" Barabbas shouted and kicked him in the side, sending him rolling across the ground. "Get up and kill me."

Coughing and heaving for air, Malon couldn't speak. He shook his head. Why would Barabbas want to die? What possessed him?

Leaving Malon gasping, Barabbas bolted over and jerked Topaz from the other man's grasp. He dangled her by one leg, and her tiny, helpless cry pierced the night air.

"Don't you care about your sister? Do you want me to kill her?" His nose and mouth twitched sporadically.

"Don't…harm…her. Please." Malon staggered to his feet and extended an arm to the babe.

Barabbas jerked her out of his reach, her squalls intensifying. When Imah rushed forward, he dropped Topaz into her arms, and then whirled on Malon.

Their swords clashed. Barabbas's blows came mindless, hard, and swift. He lifted his blade, his tainted face scrunching as he mustered strength to deliver a crushing strike.

Malon spun as his sword swooped and clanked against the stones. He slammed the hilt of his sword down on Barabbas's wrist, and his opponent's sword clattered to the ground. Kicking it out of reach, Malon pressed the blade against the outlaw's throat.

"Do it," Barabbas commanded through clenched teeth.

Malon drew in deep breaths to control his pain, and

then stepped back. "No."

Barabbas's fierce features wilted. "Why not? Do you know how many people I have killed? I will kill your family if you leave me the chance."

"Yes, you should have died. But Jesus suffered in your place. He died in your stead. How can I take the life he died to save?"

"No. He didn't die to save me. The people chose me. He died his own death."

"The people hate you. You terrorize them. Jesus was innocent. He didn't have to die. He laid his life down willingly. You must have witnessed that when you saw him standing in Pilate's hall."

The twitching of Barabbas's mouth and nose resumed, but he clamped his lips tight.

Malon breathed deep, and then pressed on. Where this boldness came from, he couldn't imagine. "There was something different about him, wasn't there?"

Barabbas's hands fell limp at his sides. "Never have I seen a man like him."

"He was different, because he was the Messiah. He possessed God's love. He took your cross and died willingly so you could go free."

"I was glad he died. I've never been afraid of anything, but I feared the calm sacrifice in Jesus' eyes." The outlaw's hands trembled as he lifted a finger and pointed at Malon. "I thought he was dead, but I see him shining through your eyes."

"That's because he is alive. He rose from the dead as the Scriptures promised. There's no need to fear him. He died for you because he loves you."

"No, he didn't die for me. His blood is not on my hands."

"His death was not to bring guilt upon you, but to free you from it. Just as Pilate set you free because Jesus took your place, God can pardon you because Jesus' blood paid the penalty for your sin."

When Malon paused, emotions played across his enemy's face. He wasn't sure where the words came from, but he was grateful he'd known what to say. "Barabbas, you are free to go. You don't have to be held captive by hate and greed any longer."

"I have heard enough of this. Come on, men. Let's go."

His men glanced from one to the other as Barabbas turned toward the gate, leaving his sword where it dropped.

"What? We're leaving?" The man who had seized Topaz whirled on Barabbas. "You're not going to kill him?"

Barabbas looked at Malon, then at the floor. "No."

"You coward! He killed my brothers in that fire. He

caused your burns. This dog deserves to die a painful death, followed by his family."

"Leave him, Peretz. This man is protected by God."

Peretz spun to face Malon, hate radiating from his eyes. "I won't leave while he yet lives."

His leader's black eyes narrowed. "You dare challenge me, boy? I said leave him."

Peretz raised his sword and raced toward Malon. Barabbas dove between them, and Peretz's sword pierced Barabbas's chest, the force of his attack sending them both tumbling to the ground.

Malon stood frozen as Peretz jumped up and tried to dislodge the sword from Barabbas's chest. It stuck fast. Breathing heavily, Barabbas tilted his head and stretched his arm, grasping for his blade, still just out of his reach.

With both hands, Peretz gripped the hilt protruding from his leader's chest. He groaned as he pulled, and in a sickening gush of blood, the blade tore free. He locked his gaze on Malon, the hate in his eyes promising death. Then his eyes grew wide. The air whooshed from his lungs, and he toppled backward. The tip of Barabbas's sword protruded from his stomach as he fell next to his killer.

Malon's gaze dropped to Barabbas wheezing on the cold stones. He rushed forward and knelt beside him. Placing his hands gently beneath Barabbas's head, he raised it to ease his breathing. Tears spilled from his eyes as blood trickled from Barabbas's mouth. This was the man he'd spent the years hating, and now—

"There," Barabbas rasped. "Now Jesus and I…are…even." He let out his final breath, and his dark eyes glazed over.

Malon brushed Barabbas's eyelids closed and rose, tears blurring the images around him. Imah's sobs were muffled into Abba's shoulder as she clung tightly to Topaz.

When he faced Barabbas's band, they shrunk back as if he would strike them. Then, watching him with caution, backed away and slipped into the night.

"What is that smell?" Abba sniffed.

"Smoke?" Malon's brows knit. "But we stopped Barabbas in time." So what could…? He looked up into the night sky. A gray haze hindered his view of the stars. "Unless—"

"Tyrus!" A pound on the gate startled him. Abba threw it open to Uncle Noah. He stood there panting, and soot streaked his face. "The shop. It's on fire."

Malon followed his father and uncle as they dashed toward the market. A red glow lit the street, brightening as they drew nearer. The acrid scent of burning wood and oil permeated the air.

Neighbors ran to and fro with water pots and buckets, sloshing the contents on the flames. Though the shop was lost, they had to control the fire before it burned the entire village. Abba and Uncle Noah joined the water line.

After tearing off his cloak, Malon dunked it in a bucket of water. He rushed toward the flames spreading to the straw of the next canopy and smothered them with the fabric. He slung the cloak over and over until his muscles ached and heat singed away the hair on his arms.

By the time they doused the last flames, the sun was beginning to lighten the horizon. He was so weary and relieved he could collapse right there and sleep for weeks.

Abba surveyed the charred remains. "What are we going to do? And Kish, what will he do? Half of this was his."

"I don't think you'll be hearing from him any time soon."

Frowning, Abba turned to Malon. "What do you mean?"

"While I was in Jerusalem, I asked Peter to baptize me in the name of Jesus. Kish saw it and wasn't pleased. I haven't seen him since."

"He abandoned you in Jerusalem with the entire caravan?"

"Yes, sir."

"Then...how did you get here? Are all the goods left unattended in the Cardo?"

"A few of the disciples agreed to watch the booth for me until I return. I came as quickly as possible, because I'd been warned of Barabbas's coming. Thank the Lord I arrived in time."

"So, you must return to Jerusalem?"

"As soon as possible."

Abba let out a long sigh and ran his fingers through his dark curls. "I still don't know what we're going to do. We're ruined for sure."

"Come to Jerusalem with me."

"Jerusalem? What would we do there?"

"Jesus' disciples live together with all things common. We could sell what we have left, take the money to the disciples, and join them."

"Leave Capernaum?"

"Abba, I want to help Peter spread the gospel of Christ to men like Barabbas. I want to be amongst them."

"Then you would move to Jerusalem, with or without us."

"If I may have your blessing."

"Your savta and my family."

"We could visit often. Abba, I would so much rather have you, Imah, and Topaz near me."

"Allow me to think on it. To pray. Right now, we need sleep, and your burns need tending."

Abba was right. They didn't have any business making a decision on something so important now. With one last glance at what had been their shop, they started up the street toward home. At least that, and his family, had survived

Chapter Seventeen

Malon tied down the crates and trunks in the back of the cart while Imah scuttled around the house, fretting about forgetting something. He couldn't blame her for being flustered. Their decision to move to Jerusalem and join the believers there was a hasty one. In the month since the fire, Abba found a buyer for the house, and Uncle Noah purchased their shop property. Peter was overjoyed they'd be joining them and assured them there would be plenty of room. The thought of moving sent Malon's stomach fluttering with excitement. It was a stride toward a life of fulfillment. But he felt for Imah. To her it must be frightening.

Abba exited with another crate. "I think this is the last one. She'll have to scrape paint off the walls to take anything more."

Malon arranged the crate and retied the ropes to stabilize them on their journey. "Are we ready to go then?"

"Aaliyah," Abba called over his shoulder. "Everything is ready. We need to get started or we won't make it any distance before dusk."

She stepped out of the door, but lingered on the threshold. Bouncing Topaz in her arms. "I can't believe we're leaving. It seems all a dream."

Abba took her hand and pulled her close to his side. "HaShem has new things prepared for us. Though it seems frightening, we can trust Him."

She leaned into his shoulder and smiled up at him. "I am trying, but I've never known anywhere but Galilee. I can't imagine living in a large city like Jerusalem."

"Shall we pray before we start our journey?" Malon hated to end their intimate moment, but they really did need to get going. If they continued this way, it would take them all year to get to Jerusalem.

"Lord, we are stepping out in faith by moving to Jerusalem. We ask that You would go with us, protect us on our journey, and bless us in our new home. Amen." With the simple prayer, Abba helped Imah into the cart and climbed up beside her.

Malon walked behind them, leading the other donkey laden with belongings. By nightfall, they reached Mount

Tabor and stopped to rest. He helped Abba set up their tent while Imah built the fire to prepare supper. The plain cakes weren't his favorite, but it would be a welcome meal after a long day of travel.

Once Abba and Imah climbed inside the tent with Topaz to settle in for the night, Malon sat beside the fire, staring at the stars. He'd always loved looking into the night sky. So many stars. The vastness of them was beyond comprehension. God promised Father Abraham that his seed would be as many. Truly, Israel was as many as the stars. But over the years, their lights had dimmed. They needed to know the Messiah had come to set them free, to fill them with power, and to make all things new. Jesus had come to shine new light into this dark world, and Malon wanted to share his light with any who would listen.

He still had so much to learn. While in Jerusalem, he'd spent hours sitting at Peter's feet asking him questions about Jesus, the prophesies, the commands Jesus left them. The more he heard, the more he hungered to learn.

Morning dawned bright and clear. He stoked the fire and packed his blankets. Topaz fussed inside the tent, so he made the cakes himself.

As he was taking them off the fire, Imah emerged and flashed him a grateful smile. "How is it God has blessed me with such a son?"

He smiled back. "Never was there a more deserving mother."

Abba ducked out of the tent, swinging Topaz in his cradled arms. She giggled and cooed, so he repeated the process, with the same effect. Her baby laughter was so precious, that all within earshot wore a smile.

When at last Abba's fatherly delight was full, he surrendered the babe to her mother and took a cake from Malon. "Best to get an early start."

They finished their meal quickly and worked to get their camp packed up and ready to move. Within an hour, they were headed down the road. Keeping this pace, they'd make it to Jerusalem ahead of schedule.

The sun hadn't climbed a handbreadth above the hazy horizon when another traveler appeared down the road. As the figure grew larger, Malon cringed. A Roman with a familiar smirk carried a bundle on his back. Swallowing his disdain, Malon managed a smile. "Good morning, Gallus. Looks like you're traveling early as well."

"Yes. On my way to Cana. Though with this," he jerked a thumb at his pack, "it may take me all day to get there."

Malon exhaled, knowing where this would lead. "Sorry to hear that. It does look heavy."

"Well then, why don't you pack it for me for a while? A strapping boy like you is just what I need."

Abba cast him a disdaining glance. How was it Romans always picked the worst times to constrain a man? But...Malon's heart smote him. Wouldn't he want someone to help him if it were the other way around? How was he to show light in the world unless he served, even when it wasn't convenient?

"Of course, Centurion. Give me just a moment."

Abba's mouth dropped open. So did Gallus'.

Malon tied the donkey to the back of the cart and gave its haunches a pat. "Will you be all right, Abba?"

"Yes, but..." He fumbled with the reins. "What about you? Traveling all that way on your own? Do you want us to wait for you?"

A chuckle escaped Malon's lips before he constrained it. "I travel long distances on caravans all the time. I'll be fine. No need to drag out your trip on my account. You best get Imah and Topaz to safety as soon as possible." He stepped up on the cart wheel and gave his mother a peck on the cheek. "I'll see you in Jerusalem. Soon."

After giving Topaz's chin a pinch, he slipped his arms through the ropes on the centurion's pack. "Shall we go, Centurion of the Imperial Army?"

Gallus stuttered and followed Malon as he headed

down the road toward Cana…in the opposite direction of Jerusalem.

The centurion untangled his tongue as he wiped sweat from his neck. "So, the whole devout Jewish family is taking a pilgrimage to the Holy City."

Unsure as to whether or not he should volunteer their circumstances, Malon chuckled and replied, "One might call it that." He gave Gallus a sidelong glance. "You seem to travel a lot, Centurion."

The man's face flamed a fiery red. "What's wrong with that? Should not a centurion be allowed to travel where he likes?"

"True enough." Malon leaned back to balance the weight on his back as they ambled down a hill. "Except most centurions I know have a post at a garrison and are unable to leave it. At least, not often."

"Well, I am not like other centurions." He looked away, closing the conversation that so ruffled his pompous feathers.

They continued in silence. Today's hike was much more pleasant than the last few. The weather was cooler, the scenery fresh, and not having his back lacerated by Gallus' whip helped too.

"With all this conversation, I've lost track of paces." Gallus stopped and planted his hands on his hips. "I think you've paid your mile."

All this conversation…?

Malon bit his lip and kept going. "We're not to Cana yet."

"What?"

Craning his neck, he met Gallus' perplexed gaze. "Cana. Isn't that your destination?"

"Yes, but—"

"Then we aren't there yet. I know this area as if it were my own courtyard. A mile and half, maybe two, yet to go."

Malon strode on, and a moment later, Gallus' jogging steps caught up with him. Malon kept looking down the road, concentrating on Gallus' destination. And his. The thought of returning to Jerusalem—for good this time—made his heart applaud. There was so much to do. So many people were eager to hear the gospel. He had even more to learn from Peter and the other disciples.

"You're humming." Gallus crossed his thick arms over his silver breastplate as he sauntered along.

"Was I? I'm sorry. I didn't notice. I will try to keep quiet if it bothers you."

"What is the song? A good drinking ballad?"

"Not in the least. It's a Psalm from the Scriptures. 'I have trusted in Thy mercy; my heart shall rejoice in Thy salvation.'"

"So your God is a merciful character."

"Merciful to those who love and reverence Him. Fearful to those who do not."

"You are a strange people."

Malon grinned. "I suppose we might seem so."

They walked on. The sun grew warmer as it rose in the sky. His brow dripped with sweat. He shifted the pack so most of the weight rested on his left shoulder. His right was aching.

When at last the city of Cana came into sight, Gallus stopped. "All right, you've carried it far enough."

"We've several furlongs yet to go to reach the city."

"I'll take the pack from here."

Unease flickered over the centurion's features, so Malon complied. He did want to head toward Jerusalem. He still had two days to travel.

"As you wish, Centurion." Slipping his arms free of the rope straps, he lowered the pack to the ground and stretched.

Gallus stood with his arms folded across his chest. Disdain glimmered in his eyes as he looked down his pointy nose at Malon.

"With as much as you despise Jews, I am surprised you allow one to carry your things. Do we not contaminate your belongings?"

"Are you still a Jew?"

Malon's head tilted. What an odd question. "Of course I am. I was born a Jew." Why would he ask something so senseless? "You knew without a second glance I was a Jew before. Why do you ask now?"

The centurion removed his helmet and wiped the sweat from his brow. "Something has changed. You're different. You don't have the same Jewish pride and stubbornness."

A frown darkened Malon's vision. He gaped at the centurion.

"The last several times you carried my pack, you were obstinate. Just like every other Jew. You trudged out your thousand steps and dropped the pack, heading for home like a pigeon. This time, you have carried my pack nearly four miles — and willingly." Gallus raised his chin and narrowed his eyes. "What's wrong with you, boy?"

"I…" For once, he didn't know what to say. Truly, he was different. He'd felt different since Peter had taken him into that little room and prayed over him after baptizing him. So then Gallus' question was merited. He was yet a Jew, but he was different from most Jews because he followed Jesus of Nazareth as the Christ. How did one explain such a difference to a Roman?

"I am a follower of Jesus."

"The Nazarene who was crucified?"

"Yes, the Jesus that was crucified, buried, and resurrected by the power of God."

Gallus' brows shot up. "Ah, so you believe he has risen from the dead?"

"I know he has. His power changed me."

The centurion kicked a pebble, and it bounced down the lane and into a bush, startling a quail. "Well, if it makes you a more willing bearer of my pack, I won't try to change your mind. No matter how ridiculous the notion. You may go now."

Malon gave him a smile and turned toward Jerusalem. He was already tired and aching, but the journey would be a lighthearted one. He could travel quickly on his own, and his family awaited him.

The thought of his mother and father joining the believers thrilled his heart. Together, they would work along with Peter and the other disciples to spread the good news of Christ to all Israel.

He quickened his pace as if a magnet drew him toward the Holy City, a force beyond his control. Sounds reverberated around him — the Judean breeze, birds, locusts, his footsteps on the gravel path…. But he stopped, listening to something inaudible to everyone else. It echoed inside his heart.

Freely I have given to you, freely give. Put forth your hands and share what I have given you. There are sinners who must be changed, captives who must be freed, and men groping in darkness who need you to shed the light. I have placed my call in your heart. Now open it up and call out to others.

Epilogue

Malon never forgot those first few weeks in Jerusalem. He never got a chance to express his thanks to Stephen and tell him what resulted from his dream, because Stephen was stoned by an angry mob days before Malon and his family returned. Great mourning amongst the believers for his loss accompanied an equally great joy. Stephen had kept the faith and died for the name of Jesus Christ. That was an honor.

When Peter was called to Caesarea, Malon accompanied him to the house of Cornelius the centurion. There he found a new love for the harbor city. He returned a short time later with Phillip and shared the gospel with his uncle Tavor. Over the next years, he made frequent visits to preach to the growing number of believers there. Because of his uncle's shipping business, he often spent time at the docks and discovered a new outreach to the immigrants and sailors. After taking Petronilla as his bride, Malon moved to Caesarea and purchased a house near the docks. Together, he and Petronilla stood like Herod's lighthouse, shedding the good news to all who would listen. God blessed them with six children, five sons and a daughter, who carried on their missionary work, even after the Roman conquest of Jerusalem.

Malon and his family traveled to Capernaum several times a year to visit Savta and his aunt and uncles. They discovered Kish had set up a shop across the market from their former location. Uncle Noah always suspected Kish, not Barabbas's men, started the fire. Malon and Tyrus chose to ignore his claims that Kish opened his shop only weeks after the fire with some of the exact goods they'd had in their shop the night the flames were kindled.

Tyrus and Aaliyah abided in Jerusalem and served the church faithfully. Several times, they were beaten and jailed for the Gospel's sake. At the age of sixty-nine, Tyrus was beaten for his faith the last time. He perished from the wounds. Aaliyah died shortly thereafter, considering her work on earth fulfilled. Six months later, Titus besieged Jerusalem.

Topaz grew up among the believers in Jerusalem, but at sixteen, she joined her brother in Caesarea. She married one of Phillip's sons and bore him nine children.

Because of the testimony and faith of Tyrus, Aaliyah, and their family, countless souls received the good news of Christ. Following the example of their Messiah, they served the church with vigor and joy.

The End.

Don't miss the rest of the Days of

Messiah Series!

Volume I – The Healer's Touch
Volume II – The Messiah's Sign
Volume III – The Master's Calling

Thank you for reading! We hope you enjoyed the journey.

If you enjoyed The Master's Calling, please consider leaving a review on Amazon, Goodreads and your favorite sites. Telling your friends about the book is the best compliment you can give to an author.

You can contact the author and keep up with her new releases by connecting with her on the following links

Facebook: www.facebook.com/AuthorAmberSchamel

Twitter: @AmberSchamel

Pintrest: www.pintrest.com/AmberDSchamel

or on www.AmberSchamel.com

Glossary and Pronunciation Guide

*Hebrew Pronunciation note: the 'ch' sound in most Hebrew words makes a sound like the "ch" in "Bach". It's a throat sound, and literally almost sounds like you're clearing your throat with almost a "Ha" sound. This sound will be symbolized by a star followed by a ch. (*ch)

Aaliyah (uh-LEE-uh)

Hebrew name meaning "to rise above".

Abba (AH-bah)

Hebrew for "father".

Adonai (Ah-d-oh-NIE)

Hebrew word for "The Lord".

Barabbas (Bar-AH-Bah-s)

A notable murderer and thief who was taken prisoner by the Romans. He was then released instead of

Jesus. Referenced in Matt. 27, Mark 15, Luke 23 and John 18.

Chag Semeach (*Ch-AH-g S-ah-ME-a*ch)

Hebrew expression meaning "Happy Festival" or "Happy Passover."

Chaim (*Ch-AH-yeem)

Hebrew name meaning "life".

Elohim (El-lo-HEEM)

Hebrew word for God meaning "Creator" or "Judge".

El Roi (El R-oh-EE)

Hebrew name for God meaning "The God who sees".

Hannah (H-AN-uh)

Fictional name for Simon Peter's wife. Referenced in Matt 8:14, Mark 1:30 and Luke 4:38.

HaShem (H-AH-shem)

Hebrew name for God meaning "The Name".

Imah (EE-mah)

Hebrew for "mother".

Jehovah Jireh (Ye-ho-VAH YEE-rey)

Hebrew name for God meaning "God will Provide."

Ken (K-EH-n)

Hebrew word for "yes".

Kish (K-IH-sh)

Hebrew name meaning "Bird catcher". Can also mean "Difficult, for age."

Malon (MAH-lone)

Alternate spelling of Mahlon, the name of Ruth's first husband. The name in Hebrew means "pardon" or can also mean "infirmity".

Mazel Tov (Ma-zel TOE-v)

Hebrew phrase used to express congratulations, usually for a happy or significant occasion or event.

Menorah (Me-NO-rah)

A candle or lamp stand used in the temple with seven branches. The menorah was often depicted in Jewish art, architecture and used in festivals such as Hanukah.

Mezuzah (Meh-ZOO-zah)

A scroll, often in a decorative case, inscribed with verses of the Torah, specifically Deut. 6:4-9 and 11:13-21. A mezuzah is affixed to the doorpost of Jewish homes to remind them of the Law of the Lord.

Musht (M-UH-sh-t)

A fish commonly caught from the Sea of Galilee. It is often eaten by the locals and today is referred to as Saint Peter's Fish. Also known as Blue Tilapia.

Petronilla (Petron-il-la)

Traditional name attributed to Simon Peter's

daughter.

Savta (S-AH-v-tah)

Hebrew for "grandmother".

Shabbat Shalom (Shab-BOT Sha-LO-m)

Hebrew greeting for the Sabbath. Literally
"Peaceful Sabbath"

Simon (S-EYE-mon)

Simon later known as Peter was the son of Jonah,
brother of Andrew. He and his brother were Jesus'
disciples. The gospel of Mark is said to be his account.

Shofar (Show-FA-r)

A type of trumpet made of ram's horn.

Tallit (Ta-LEET)

Hebrew prayer shawl used to cover the head of
male worshipers during prayer and Torah reading.

Tavor (Tah-VOR)

Hebrew name meaning "misfortune".

Tiltan (Til-TAN)

Hebrew name meaning "clover, shamrock".

Topaz (TOE-paz)

Hebrew name meaning "precious stone".

Tyrus (TIE-rus)

Biblical name meaning "Rock, sharp". Ezekiel 27:3
refers to Tyrus as being a merchant, which is why I chose

this name for the character. *And say unto Tyrus, O thou that art situate at the entry of the sea, which art a merchant of the people for many isles, Thus saith the Lord God; O Tyrus, thou hast said, I am of perfect beauty.*

Tzivyah (Tz-iv-EE-yah)

Hebrew name meaning "deer".

Yahweh (YAH-way)

Hebrew name for God meaning "You are the Lord".

*****

28426740R10144

Made in the USA
San Bernardino, CA
28 December 2015